ChangelingPress.com

Hero/Snow Duet
A Hounds of Hell MC Romance
Jamie Targaet

Hero/Snow Duet
A Hounds of Hell MC Romance
Jamie Targaet

All rights reserved.
Copyright ©2024 Jamie Targaet

ISBN: 978-1-60521-930-1

Publisher:
Changeling Press LLC
315 N. Centre St.
Martinsburg, WV 25404
ChangelingPress.com

Printed in the U.S.A.

Editor: Crystal Esau
Cover Artist: Bryan Keller

Table of Contents

Hero (Hounds of Hell MC 1)
A Hounds of Hell MC Romance
Jamie Targaet

Jade -- I came back to town because my grandmother passed away and she was the only family I had left. Grams never wanted me involved with the MCs, but I always knew my father was a member. That was all I knew about him. Now he's the president of Hounds of Hell MC. Or, as it turns out, he could also be the president of their rival MC, the Cottonmouths. Hounds of Hell MC sent one of their men, Hero, to keep me safe until my parentage gets figured out. No one is telling me why that's necessary. I should go back to Providence. But I'm done with grad school, and there's really nothing for me back there. And Hero is one beefy, gorgeous temptation of a biker. Part of me wants to stay here, in the home where I grew up. Part of me just wants *him*.

Hero -- When my prez gave me the babysitting assignment to keep an eye on the daughter he's never known, I resented it. Until I got a look at her. Choosing me to protect her was the right call. The Cottonmouths took her from me once. No one is taking her away from me again -- no matter who has to die. I don't care who her father is. Jade is mine.

Chapter One

Jade

"Are you sure you want to be doing this?"

Jaeden smiled at the kind older gentleman who'd been her grandmother's companion for the last couple of decades. Emery Phillips' round face was heavily lined, and he was missing a couple of teeth. But his blue eyes were bright and friendly. When he smiled? Yeah. She could totally see how he'd won the heart of one Mina Dock.

Her heart clenched in her chest thinking about the loss of Grams. The stubborn old woman had loved her to death. She'd been the only family Jade ever had. "I *could* sell it," she told Emery as they stood on the front porch where she'd played as a child. "But now that I'm done with grad school there's really no reason to stay in Providence. I think I'd like to settle here."

The old sign she'd made in school still stood in the flowerbed at the edge of the porch. "Gram's Garden," it read in faded red paint. And on the bottom step, if she looked closely, Jade could just make out the hash marks she'd made each time her grandmother had run off her estranged father through her childhood. Exactly seven marks. And those were the times she was aware of.

Okay, so not all her memories were happy. But as she grew older, she had a better idea why Grams did what she did. Her grandmother had tried to do what was best for her.

"He never stopped coming here, asking about you, you know," Emery went on. "Last time he was here was a couple of weeks before she died."

Jade blew out an exhale. "You were here?"

The older man shook his head.

Well, she was grown now and had just finished grad school. If her father stopped by, maybe she'd talk to him. Yeah, he was supposedly the leader of a notorious biker gang and she'd heard some wild stories through the years. But she wouldn't judge him based on that. "If he comes by, I'll handle it," Jade assured him.

Emery's gaze held a note of concern. "You get she didn't want you in their world, right? That she was trying to keep you away from that bunch?"

Jade nodded. She understood very well.

Her mother, Vanessa Dock, had a wild streak a mile wide according to Grams. As a young woman of nineteen, she fell in with the wrong crowd. She'd accidentally gotten pregnant once but lost it because she couldn't kick alcohol and drugs.

When she'd gotten pregnant with Jade, Grams had essentially placed her daughter on lockdown. Took her to rehab, to doctor visits. Her grandmother had taken care of her mother and helped her to turn her life around.

Gram's efforts paid off. Vanessa gave birth and took care of Jade. She got a job and had plans to get back to school. The three of them lived there in the home she'd inherited. They'd been happy judging by all the pictures. She just wished she could remember more.

Her mother's death in a car accident when Jade was three years old was a cruel irony.

"He tried hard to take you away from her once your mother passed," Emery explained. "Wasn't above threatening her either. Just watch yourself with them. Nothing but bad news."

Jade's confidence in talking to her father waned a little at the warning. Emery ran a bar on the outskirts of town and knew most of the locals, most especially the MCs. Was there something he wasn't telling her?

"I will," she told him, knowing he was looking out for her. "Thank you."

Emery helped her carry the few items she'd brought with her into the house. It wasn't much. The funeral was tomorrow. She had a lot to do between settling her grandmother's affairs, going through the house, and moving everything from her apartment in Providence.

She'd just finished her graduate degree in the summer session. She could participate in the fall commencement at the university back in Rhode Island, but she doubted she would. Not now. The job as research assistant ended last week, and she had a couple of weeks left on her lease to get everything moved and say her goodbyes.

They talked for a while before Emery headed back home, telling her he'd pick her up for the funeral tomorrow. And she was grateful for that, especially when she walked back into her childhood home alone.

Grams was gone.

She'd had a stroke in her sleep, they'd said. It had been quick. Emery had called her three nights before to let her know. It still broke Jade that she'd never gotten to say goodbye.

She talked to Grams each week on the phone. The last time had been two days before she passed. Her grandmother had sounded just the same. She'd been trying to plant her garden, putting up with Emery's nonsense as she worked. Never anything negative to speak of. Always ended the call with, "I'm so proud of you. I love you, Jade."

Jade didn't realize she'd started to cry. Sinking to the floor by her Grams' bed, she finally let the grief drop over her now that she was here. Now she was alone. All she had was a degree she didn't have immediate plans for, a couple of loser boyfriends, and the house that was now hers.

When she'd managed to pull herself off the floor, she found herself looking through her grandmother's bedside table. Most people kept junk in such drawers, but not Mina Dock.

There were her medications and an emery board. A couple of hair ties. Then there were the pictures.

She only had framed pictures of Jade and her mother on the table next to the lamp. In the drawer, in a small hand-sized photo album were other pictures. Private ones that must have been just for her. A picture of Jade as a baby on her mother's hip. Another of Mina and Emery, kissing under the mistletoe last Christmas.

Jade smiled. She'd taken that photo herself.

The final photo Jade hadn't seen before. A picture of her mother when she was younger, cuddled up on the lap of a man who looked very familiar. She couldn't help but stare at the picture. The man who held her was a large guy with thick waves of dark hair, hazel eyes, and a killer smile. He had a leather jacket with a wolf insignia of some type on it.

Jade's heart flew. Was he her father?

She'd always been too scared to really look at him when he showed up when she was little. Most of the time, Grams made her flee into the house like he wasn't even allowed to look at her. But the few times Jade hadn't been sent into the house, she didn't make eye contact. She tried not to move.

Grams told her he wasn't a good man. That always made her worry. What if he did take her away one day?

Jade always tried to make herself small,

unnoticeable. When she was a teenager, she didn't go outside as often so she didn't remember him coming by. But he must have.

Her father had apparently been so bad Grams wouldn't allow him near her. What had he done? It was the conversation they'd never had.

And why in twenty-four years had he never given up?

When he stopped by, and apparently, he would, how would that go?

Putting herself together again, Jade decided to head into town for takeout. She'd driven most of the day and really hadn't stopped to eat much of anything.

As she headed out to her SUV, she had no idea someone was in the shadowy corner of the property she'd inherited, watching her.

* * *

Hero

Christian Hammond, Hero to his brothers, watched from the inside of his Jeep as the leggy brunette made her way to the small SUV. She was probably heading to town, so he decided to give her a head start and see what she was up to. He didn't have anything else going on at the moment.

When Razor told him to go see if his daughter had come home, Hero had been annoyed by the assignment. What the fuck was he? A babysitter?

Now that he got a look at her, he didn't have much to complain about. Her jeans were tight, showing off legs a mile long and a nice ass to go with them. Her baggy college sweatshirt didn't do her any favors, but her long dark hair framed a face that was delicate, beautiful.

How the fuck did Razor have a daughter who

looked like *that*?

His club president probably wouldn't appreciate him ogling his only child the way he was either but... *Look at her.*

Scrubbing a hand over his beard, Hero waited as she started the car and threw on her seat belt. Finally, she started down the long gravel driveway that took her to Route 8. Hero let her reach town, not having any trouble spotting her as she parked on Main Street and headed straight for the local coffee shop.

Hero liked the way she walked with her shoulders back, her head held high. Confidence was sexy as hell on a woman and the sway of her round little ass didn't hurt either.

His phone rang before he could shut off the engine and follow her on foot. Not surprisingly, it was Razor.

"She make it into town?" he asked.

"Yeah," Hero told him. "Old man Phillips was there and talked to her for a while."

"Hmm." A pause. "I've got Snow working on the girl over at the attorney's office. She's sweet on him. We'll see if she can find out if my girl means to keep the house or sell it."

"Want me to stay on her?" As much as he'd bitched to himself about the assignment, he was minding a lot less now.

A long pause which was odd. Razor usually didn't have any trouble issuing orders.

"Yeah, man, I need you to," Razor said in a lower voice. "I'd give it to the prospects but... I need someone I can trust on this. I'm going to need eyes on her at all times until I can resolve some shit. If you'd stay on her until midnight, I'll have Snow come relieve you."

What was this about?

Hero wouldn't question his prez. He appreciated that Razor trusted him.

"I'm on it," Hero told him. "She's here in town now, so I'm keeping an eye out."

"Talk to you soon," Razor told him, ending the call.

His daughter had come home for the funeral just like Razor said she would.

Everyone in Mercy knew Mina Dock. The old woman had a lot of friends so tomorrow was bound to be a circus.

The girl's grandmother taught school for years and had retired not too long ago. She was apparently as stubborn as Razor and that was saying a lot. The president of his club had been trying for years to see his daughter, to see if Mina would agree to any type of shared custody arrangement or visitation rights. The old woman wouldn't hear of it.

Razor never talked about it. Hero had heard stories.

Razor had never taken an old lady, and the girl's mother, by all accounts, had been one of the club sluts for a time. Apparently, when she got knocked up, Mina Dock took control of the situation and that was the end of it.

Razor had a daughter he wasn't allowed to see any more than he had her mother before that. The girl's mother died a long time ago. Mina Dock had to have been one tough bitch to have kept Razor away.

Hero climbed out of his Jeep when she darted back out of the shop, a coffee cup in hand as she continued up the sidewalk. Her movements were fast, determined.

Hero grinned. *There it was.*

Razor walked like that when he meant business, or he was pissed at someone.

Speeding up a little, Hero headed in her direction. He was enjoying the sunny day, his curvy assignment. Things could certainly be worse.

When he saw a white delivery van come up the road behind him, he couldn't have said why he noticed. Three familiar-looking men jumped out and he froze.

Fucking Cottonmouths. What the fuck were *they* doing here? They weren't wearing their cuts but he knew who they were.

And he'd lost her. He didn't know which shop she'd darted into, but he moved even faster. He couldn't help but feel they were here for her, same as him.

Fuck.

While he was fairly sure he could handle the three of them on his own, he'd been in enough skirmishes to know better than to be one against three with the girl in play. He couldn't risk texting, so he called Razor back.

"Yeah."

"Three Cottonmouths just showed up," Hero said quickly. "We're on Main Street."

"Really?" Razor didn't sound amused. "The posse's coming."

"Thanks." Hero pocketed his phone and watched as the three of them darted across the street, walking in front of him on the sidewalk. They didn't even notice him.

The first one was Jimmy Jazz, a scrappy little fucker who put on a good show until things got physical. Then he tended to fade into the background like the little coward he was. The second one, Big Dog, had the tender sweetness of a pit bull and was one hell of a fighter. Hero knew he could stand toe-to-toe against the massive, shaggy-looking asshole. But he'd rather not.

The one that worried him was Baby Face.

Walking ahead of the other two, Baby Face was average size with a pretty face the girls loved. And he could draw them to him like a bee charmer, all honey and smiles.

His pretty face concealed a black heart. A more sadistic little fucker Hero hadn't met. What he lacked in size, he made up for in savagery. He was good with knives and could take most down with his blades before they even realized they were bleeding out.

He'd cut up many a club slut, too.

That they were here for Razor's daughter had him wondering what the hell was going on. Why were the Cottonmouths after the girl?

When she darted out of another shop -- he didn't know which store it was -- his heart sank to see them right on her heels. Hero sped up, hoping his backup got there fucking fast.

Baby Face called out to her. When she didn't stop, he did it again.

Don't stop.

But she did, turning to face them and her eyes widening in fear.

The van raced up then and screeched to a halt next to them. She dropped her coffee and ran. Baby Face caught her by her long dark hair, giving the other two time to snatch her off the street and quickly haul her into the back of the van.

Baby Face looked around as he climbed in himself, his gaze meeting Hero's. The bastard winked at him before slamming the van doors hard.

As Hero watched, the van sped away.

* * *

Jade

When Jade woke up, her head was pounding and her mouth was sand dry. Her vision was blurry when her eyes slit open. When she didn't recognize the room she found herself in, her heart lurched in fear. *Where was she?*

All her grandmother's warnings about MCs echoed in her mind as her eyes adjusted to the dim, dirty room with no windows. She could hear the low din of voices that didn't sound too far away.

The last thing she remembered was the three men chasing her down the sidewalk in town. It had been nothing for them to snatch her off the street and throw her in the back of their van.

When she went to sit up and fetch her phone out of her jeans pocket, she found her right wrist was hand-cuffed to the dirty cot she'd been lying on.

Why am I handcuffed? What do they want with me?

How long had she been there? Her grandmother's funeral…

She had to find a way out. Trying to stay calm as fear crept into her mind, she scanned the room around her. An old metal desk was shoved in one corner. Papers, books, old coffee cups, and assorted items were scattered all over it. Nearby was an office chair that had seen better days.

Old calendars hung on the wall, some with lewd photos of scantily clad girls. Others had photos of vintage motorcycles. All of them faded, some with stains. The most recent year was 2013 best she could make out.

The back of her head really hurt. With her free

hand, she found a lump at the back of her skull, a scab on her scalp. When she reached for her jeans pocket, she found her phone was gone. As her mind scrambled for answers, the door to the shabby little room opened. The young man who walked in wore a denim cut with a black shirt and jeans. She recognized him as one of them who'd taken her. Of course he was a biker.

In another world, she might have considered him handsome. He had blue eyes and a face any actor would beg for, all sharp cheekbones and a jawline for days. Rich locks of chestnut hair framed that face, and his smile was stunning when he turned it on her.

The smile didn't reach his eyes.

Before he could speak, two more bikers came in behind him, pushing her anxiety higher. One was tall and lanky with spiky brown hair. One was huge with shaggy hair and a scary, bearded face.

"Our friend is awake," the pretty one told them, his gaze cold on her.

"What are we going to do with her?" the shaggy one asked. "The Hounds are going to be on our ass."

The Hounds? An image of the wolf on the cut the man wore in the old picture of her mother flashed in her mind.

"Sure they are." His blue-eyed gaze stayed on her unnervingly. "Razor's always thought she was *his* kid."

"You don't even know who Razor is, do you?" he demanded of her. "Mina kept you hidden away, didn't she? But Mina's gone. She can't save you now."

Tears stung the backs of her eyes at the mention of the only family member she had left. "What do you want with me?" Jade asked. It sounded a lot braver in her head. "I'm here for the funeral. That's all."

"I know," the pretty one told her, taking a knee

next to the cot.

He was two feet away, but she was pushing herself closer to the wall, away from him.

"Hero saw us," the biker with spiked hair warned.

Hero?

"Hero ain't going to do shit!" Color flooded the leader's face as he stared at her wide-eyed. "By the time they figure out where she is…"

"Where's that?" the shaggy one asked.

"I thought Big Billy could use another girl for his club." The leader grabbed her chin roughly in his hand, turning her face to one side before she managed to shove him away. "What do you think she'll get for a night?"

Jade stared at him in shock. *Human trafficking?* She couldn't have heard him right.

"She'll be a club slut, just like her mama was," their leader continued.

Panic rioted in her mind. Grams never talked about her mother's time with the bikers. Had her mother wronged someone? Why come after *her*?

Had her mother been a prostitute? Or had she been trafficked? Not knowing the details, combined with the terror of her current situation, had her fighting to stay silent.

"I-I don't know anything about my mother," Jade said slowly. "She died when I was little. I'm sorry if she did… something…"

"You're *sorry*?" The leader laughed then, a humorless sound. "Sorry? Sorry is what you're going to be after a few weeks on your fucking back." The leer the shaggy one cut her had her stomach turning.

"What do you think boys?" he went on. "Think we should break her in for Big Billy? Give her a preview of her new life?"

The one with spiked hair cut him a look. "Ain't she your half-sister though?"

What? Oh, God. That couldn't be true, could it?

"The fuck you say to me?"

The leader was on his feet in an instant, color flooding his angry face as he spun to face his companions. The back of his cut showed a coiled-up snake looking ready to strike. *Cottonmouth* was printed on the denim above it.

Grabbing a handful of the other man's shirt, the leader slammed him against the nearest wall hard. "She's not going to be anything but a used-up whore once she's been in Billy's a while." He got in the other man's face. "That's all your dumb ass needs to know."

The man in his clutches already had his hands up. "Sorry, Baby Face. Didn't mean nothing by it. You can do whatever."

Baby Face?

"That's right." Letting the man go, he turned to face her. His face was lit up in evil glee. "We need to get her to Billy's. Tonight."

Jade didn't like the way all three of them looked her over.

"Give her another dose," Baby Face told them. "If she's strung out, she'll be easier to transport." With that, he turned on his heel and headed out of the room with the shaggy one on his heels. The other pulled out a syringe and came straight for her. She struggled, but it wasn't much of a fight.

Within minutes, Jade again greeted oblivion.

Chapter Two

Hero

That Razor himself showed up didn't entirely surprise Hero. He cut his prez a look as he joined him at his watch point at the edge of the woods. He'd followed the Cottonmouths to a familiar cabin on the edge of town. The setting sun cast eerie shadows all around them.

"What the fuck happened?" Razor demanded. Concern was etched on his heavily lined face.

Hero ducked behind the large tree. "The Cottonmouths grabbed her right off the street," Hero explained. "Before the twins got there."

At the mention of Axel and Ryder, Razor glanced at each of them in turn. "Who grabbed her?"

"Baby Face," Hero told him. "Jimmy Jazz and Big Dog."

"Fuck!" Razor scrubbed a hand through the long gray locks of his hair. "What the actual fuck is *this* about?"

"I was hoping you could tell us," Hero replied. "What do the Cottonmouths want with her?"

Hero couldn't see his eyes for the dark sunglasses he wore. When Razor glanced in the direction of the small cabin the rival MC used for deals and meetings, Hero knew he wasn't going to get an answer.

"The point is, they've *got* her." Razor blew out an exhale. "If it were Eli, I wouldn't be so worried. That kid of his?"

Hero agreed. Eli was the president of the Cottonmouths, and while he wasn't the best guy, he could at least be reasoned with. Baby Face, his son, was as unpredictable as he was sadistic. Anything could be happening to the girl. The thought made Hero's stomach drop. "What's the plan?"

No sooner than he said the words than they watched Jimmy Jazz and Big Dog carry her unconscious form out of the cabin in the direction of the van.

"Move!" Razor hissed at them.

Hero ran full speed in their direction, watching as Baby Face walked around, opening the back doors of the van. When he reached them, the twins on his heels, he pulled out his Ruger, popping Jimmy Jazz in the shoulder as he walked around from the back. Yelling, Jimmy Jazz went down.

More shots were exchanged between Hero and Big Dog, the twins firing behind him. It ended abruptly with Hero and Big Dog each pointing a gun at the other in a standoff.

"Hi, Hero," Baby Face came up behind him, the setting sunlight winking off the blade he held with the point aimed at Hero's eye.

Hero froze as a fourth guy started up the van.

"Why are you up my ass today?" Baby Face asked him with a deceptive grin.

Keeping his eye and gun trained on Big Dog, Hero replied. "You know why."

"You need to leave this one alone," Baby Face warned him. "There are things you don't understand about the situation."

"Why don't you enlighten me?" Hero stayed still, aware. He knew Razor was close by.

"I don't owe you an explanation," Baby Face told him, inching the knife closer. "You need to take your men and fuck off."

"Oh, we will, but we're taking the girl with us," Hero promised him. "And she'd better be in perfect health."

The other man's notorious temper flared. "Or *what*? It's none of your Goddamn business what I do with the little bitch. She's *not* Razor's kid. Get that through your thick skulls and *fuck off.*"

"You think she's Eli's?" Hero asked. He knew some people believed that.

Out of the corner of his eye, he saw Baby Face's cleft chin inch up in challenge.

"Funny, I don't see Eli," Hero pointed out. "He even know what you're doing?"

"Fuck you, Hero." Baby Face moved the blade until the tip pressed into his skin.

"Answer the question." Razor stood behind Baby Face, his own gun pressed into the back of the man's skull.

Pulling the knife away from Hero's face, Baby Face laughed. "So serious. All over a girl you don't know anything about."

Baby Face had balls. Hero would give him that. He turned around to face Razor, seeming unfazed by the fact that a gun was pointed at his face now.

"And you do?" Razor smirked at him. "I don't know what your game is, son. But you're not taking the girl."

"Wanna bet?" In the blink of an eye, Baby Face jabbed his knife into Razor's abdomen. The older man yelled. Hero pulled the trigger, blood spraying from Big Dog's jaw as he screamed and collapsed to the ground. He wasn't far from where Razor dropped to his knees, his hands clutched at his bleeding torso.

In horror, Hero watched a small stream of blood escape the corner of Razor's mouth. He dashed to his president's side as the van roared to life. Baby Face and Jimmy grabbed Big Dog, scrambling into the back of the van as it backed away from the cabin. The twins fired shots at it, trying to hit the tires as it spun rocks and sped away with Razor's daughter in the back.

"Axel, tail them," Hero called out. "Ryder, bring the Jeep down here. We've got to take him to the ER."

Razor was shaking his head, falling over. "Get her back," he whispered before he lost consciousness.

"I will," Hero assured him. He'd get Razor's daughter back and he'd make life hell for the Cottonmouths while he did it.

* * *

Jade

Jade awoke next in a different room. This time she wasn't chained to the bed. Her limbs felt heavy as she tried just to lift her head. What had they drugged her with?

"Hey, darlin'." A soft voice came from next to her. A pretty young woman with red hair and a lot of makeup came into her field of vision, her green eyes soft with concern. "I'm Kimmie. How are you feeling?"

Jade's gaze moved over the room, taking in the rustic-themed bedroom. The bed was huge, the bedding simple. Two lamps, a bedside table, and a mini-bar below the enormous TV mounted on the wall. Another door was open, a bathroom. "Where am I?"

Kimmie seemed confused. "Big Billy's?"

"What's that?"

"I fucking knew it," Kimmie said under her breath, taking a seat next to her on the bed. "It's a biker club, sweetie. We were told you knew you were coming here."

Jade shook her head. "I've been kidnapped." She tried to fight back her escalating fear. "I'm in town for my grandmother's funeral."

Kimmie concealed her alarm quickly. "You have family around here?"

"I grew up in Mercy," she explained.

"Any of that family wrong any of the MCs?"

What did she say? Maybe truth was best. Especially since she appeared to be in very real danger. "I think," Jade said slowly, "my father is in an MC."

"Which one?" Kimmie asked.

"I think he's a… wolf or…"

"Is he a Hell Hound?" she asked.

Jade nodded. "I think so. Yes."

"Who is he?"

"I don't know, honestly. My grandmother never let me see him or talk to him."

Kimmie's brows inched up. "The same grandmother who died?"

Jade nodded.

"That's not helpful," Kimmie told her. "Your grandmother steal from that MC? Wrong them in some way?"

"No." Jade frowned at her. "No. She was a very decent woman."

"Did *you* wrong them in some way?"

"I don't even know any of them!" Jade hated the panic in her own voice, her heart racing in fear. "I'm sorry. I'm trying to understand what's going on. I just want to go to my grandmother's funeral."

When tears filled her eyes, more frustration than anything, Kimmie studied her.

"Why am I here?" she asked Kimmie.

Blowing out an exhale, the other woman's gaze locked with hers. "Billy's a Cottonmouth. He owns this place. He runs pussy and drugs."

Pussy.

"We were told you were here to pay off a debt,"

Kimmie told her. "Something owed to Billy."

Panic gripped her. "You mean prostitution?"

Kimmie slowly nodded. "Yeah. I mean it's *like* that. Most of us are paid pretty good. Sometimes you get lucky, and someone likes you enough to make you their old lady. Then you don't have to be a club slut anymore."

Jade knew she was staring at the other woman like she had two heads. "I don't want to be involved with the MCs at all. I don't even know what an old lady is."

Kimmie shook her head.

"Please, you have to help me," Jade begged her. "I have to get out of here. I want to go to my grandmother's funeral. She's the only family I've got."

Sighing, Kimmie nodded. "Okay. We need to calm you down, darlin'."

When Kimmie produced a needle, jabbing it into her arm, Jade cried out in dismay. "No more drugs!" But her mind began to spin as those drugs flowed through her veins. Her vision grew blurry, and she didn't feel right. *Am I going to survive this*?

"You're supposed to start tonight," Kimmie explained, her face swimming in and out of Jade's vision. "I want to help you, but I don't want to hurt my own position here… I'll see what I can do."

* * *

Hero

Hero fished his phone out of his pocket the moment it started humming. Razor was still in surgery, and he was in the waiting room, hoping his prez made it through this. Hero saw the caller was Axel. "Speak."

"They took her to Big Billy's," Axel said without preamble.

"What?" Hero considered that for a minute. "Do you mean she's in the bar or…"

"Nope. Baby Face took her in there to *work*," Axel told him.

"Fuck me," Hero muttered. He'd been trying to reach Snow, to see if he'd go help Axel because he didn't want to leave Razor. So far there had been no word. The club's vice president was probably the best one to deal with the situation. But Razor trusted *him*. He'd told Hero to get her back.

The girl knew nothing about their world. And Baby Face had taken her to Big Billy's to be trafficked? "Stay right there," Hero told Axel, his mind made up. "I'll be there fast as I can."

"You got it."

Scrubbing a hand through his hair, Hero considered his actions. On his way out of the waiting room, out of the hospital, he tried Snow again. This time his VP answered. "Hey, how's Razor?"

"We have a situation," Hero told him, climbing into his Jeep. "I need you here at the hospital for when Razor comes out of surgery."

"Okay," Snow said.

"Can you pick up Ryder at the old Reid cabin?"

"I can," Snow replied. "Anything else I can do?"

"I'll let you know." Cutting off the call, Hero started the engine and zipped off. It would take him almost an hour to reach Big Billy's. He didn't want to let Razor down.

* * *

Once they had Axel's bike and cut loaded into the back of his Jeep, Hero met his gaze. "You ready?"

Axel nodded. "As I'm gonna be."

Hero motioned him on, waiting in the shadows as his friend scoped out the bikes parked outside Big

Billy's. All of them belonged to Cottonmouths. All they needed was for one to have the keys left in it. Otherwise, they would need a different diversion.

But there was one. Axel pointed to it before climbing on the older Harley. It didn't matter who it belonged to. Axel started it up, started racing around the gravel lot outside the bar. It took a moment before anyone reacted to the commotion he caused. Eventually, a couple of guys ran out yelling, and then Axel took off for the road, hauling ass for the highway.

It was hard not to laugh watching them run out of the bar, some hauling up their pants on their way. Staying hidden behind the utility shed out back, he waited until all but one bike was left before he made his way around to the front.

The Cottonmouths would recognize him, but he'd never personally been in Big Billy's. Without his cut, the women working in the club might not put it together. When he walked into the bar, he spotted one lone Cottonmouth passed out at his table. He recognized the old-timer but couldn't have said what his name was.

"Hey, darlin'." A cute redhead grinned at him from behind the bar. "What can I do you for?"

Hero grinned. "I'll take a beer for starters."

Pulling out a mug, she poured him a drink from the tap.

"What else?" she asked when she brought it to him. "Something else you'd like?"

Hero took a long drink from his beer. "Something brunette with long legs."

Her brows inched up at that, but she nodded. "I may be able to help you with that too."

"Yeah?"

"Yeah," she told him. "She's new and

nervous…" Seeming to consider her words, she placed her clasped hands on the bar between them, leaned in closer. "The boss gave her something to help her relax and it hit her hard."

Hero had to fight to keep his smile in place. *Fuckers.* They'd drugged her. "That doesn't pose a problem," he told her. "How much?"

Her smile faded a little, but she nodded. "Five hundred."

Pulling out his wallet, Hero fished out five hundred-dollar bills and slid them across the counter to her. As he watched, she folded the bills, tucking them away in her bra.

"Let me know when you're ready," she told him with a wink.

The redhead lingered around the counter as Hero finished his beer. Pulling out his phone, he got a text off to Snow. The answering text indicated Razor was still in surgery.

Not wanting to take any more time than he needed, Hero finished the mug and caught the young woman's gaze. "Okay."

Motioning him to follow her, she led him down a narrow side hallway by the bathrooms. The door at the end of the hall led to another area, many other doors in a bigger space. She took him to the first door on the left.

* * *

Jade

Jade felt like the room was spinning around her when Kimmie walked back in.

She wasn't alone.

A spike of fear shot through Jade's heart to see the tall man approach the bed she was lying on.

Kimmie locked the door behind them. Dark blonde hair framed a handsome face in longer waves. His beard was a shade darker. He wasn't wearing a biker's cut, but he had a sleeve of tattoos on his left arm. His black T-shirt clung to his muscular frame, his jeans tight. His blue eyes were intent on her, roaming over her in a way that had her blood running cold.

How could this be happening?

"Hey, darlin'," Kimmie leaned over her, grinning. "I found a nice looking one for your first."

Holy shit! That's what she was afraid of. But when she lifted her head, the spinning was worse, and she felt so heavy.

"She's really drugged, huh?" the biker asked, even as he sat on the edge of the bed next to her.

Jade tried with everything in her to inch away from him. It was pitiful really. When his large hand landed on her denim-covered thigh, she felt tears sting the backs of her eyes.

"She was nervous, is all," Kimmie explained, pulling a chair from its place next to the minibar to one side of the bed.

When she took a seat, the man's brows shot up. "You runnin' a two-for-one special?" he asked.

Kimmie's hands twisted in her lap. "I'm *not* part of the deal unless you're paying extra," she explained carefully. "I'd just feel better keeping an eye on things… at least at first."

The man didn't appear to appreciate that. "Having an audience isn't one of my kinks."

Kimmie looked more uncomfortable by the second. Jade took her hesitation as a slim bit of hope. Was she rethinking helping them traffic her? "Look, you're not a Cottonmouth and I know most of the others they allow in here," she explained.

"I'm a friend of Eli's," he said casually.

Jade didn't understand what that meant but it must have made a difference. Kimmie slid to the edge of the chair, nodded. "I'll just stay a minute then," she said finally.

Shaking his head, he turned his attention to Jade. Weakly, she put up her hands to ward him off. His gaze moved over her hair, her face. That hand slid up her thigh, over one breast and up to her hair. His fingers slid through her hair carefully. The spicy notes of his cologne invaded her senses. "You're brand new, aren't you?" he asked.

Humiliation lit up her face. She didn't have a response for that.

That hand traced back the way it came. Jade panicked when it disappeared under the hem of her sweatshirt. His fingers were rough on her skin, sliding over her ribs. She jerked, trying to avoid his touch, but her movements were sluggish.

He leaned closer until his lips were inches from hers. "*Shh.*"

Jade tried to dodge his kiss but wasn't fast enough. He kept it light, his lips warm and soft, lightly dancing over hers. That hand under her sweatshirt inched up toward her breast.

The irony had her heart crashing in her chest. She'd been a wallflower in college, terrified by all the horror tales of girls being drugged at parties and raped. She stuck with just two boyfriends, neither of which were great choices for her. *Look at me now.*

When those heated lips, the soft scruff of his beard, blazed a trail over her jaw to the sensitive spot beneath her ear, she again tried to move. To do *anything.*

With an impatient huff, he grabbed the hem of

her sweatshirt and swiftly yanked it up and off her body, leaving her in her plain-Jane bra. His lips continued their campaign, blazing a trail down her neck. Planting her hands on the hard wall of his chest, she tried in vain to push him away from her. When one large palm slid over a breast, she knew a moment of panic even though his touch was careful, light.

When his teeth lightly nipped at the base of her throat, Jade sucked in a breath, trying to ignore the pleasant sensations his touch invoked. Surely it was whatever they'd given her.

He moved over her, pressing himself in between her thighs and grinding the heated length of himself inside her. Despite the situation, her thighs tightened around his hips. Her back arched slightly before she thought to still her movements.

Out of the corner of her eye, she saw Kimmie rise from the chair, not meeting her gaze. Quietly, the other woman headed for the door. She was abandoning her. That more than anything had tears sliding from the corners of her eyes as the man above her continued to drop kisses over her neck and chest, pawing at her.

The sound of the door closing again made her heart sink.

A beat later, the man she'd been left with slowly lifted his head. His gaze met hers. "Are you okay?" he asked quietly.

"What do you care?" she had to ask, her voice sounding weaker than she would have liked.

"I'm going to get you out of here," he whispered.

Jade was confused and afraid to hope.

"Do you understand me?"

She managed a nod. "Why?"

"Your father sent me," he told her. "I promised him I'd get you back."

She stared at him. When he pulled his hand away from her breast, she froze.

"Will you help me?"

Did she have a choice?

Moving closer, he wrapped an arm around her shoulders. "Can you sit up?"

With help, she managed it. He handed her the sweatshirt, helped her put it on. He leaned down to get on eye level with her, his gaze searching hers. "They dosed you good, didn't they? Fuckers," he muttered.

It seemed easy enough for him to rise from the bed and haul her up and over one of his shoulders. Jade wanted to close her eyes, the motion making her feel ill, as he made his way to the door. One strong arm locked around her thighs, holding her to him. Whoever he was, he made it out of the room and into a bigger area. The air was cooler here as he headed through another door, through a smaller hallway that was covered in old-fashioned wood paneling.

"Hey!" Kimmie called as he made a beeline for the front door. Jade watched in alarm as she rushed toward them. "You can't take her out of here!" Kimmie yelled, looking panicked.

"I'm going to," he informed her.

"I'm going to be in so much trouble if you take her out of here," Kimmie whined.

"You're going to be in a lot more trouble if I *don't* take her out of here. She's protected by another MC."

The redhead looked uncertain. When he started walking again, she ran around to get ahead of him. "What am I supposed to tell them?" Jade heard her ask.

"Angel, I don't give a fuck." He sounded impatient. "Do me a favor and give me a five-minute lead, yeah?"

Jade felt something like real hope when he carried her out into the night, through a strangely empty parking lot. He didn't stop until he reached an older black Jeep, opening one of the rear doors and helping her into the back seat. It wasn't like she could fight him. "Stay down," he warned. "We're leaving."

Nodding, she lay there with her heart racing in her chest. If he was telling her the truth, maybe she'd be okay. She'd survive.

Chapter Three
Hero

Hero chuckled to see the twins walk into the clubhouse, both wearing shit-eating grins. Most of the leading members of the Mercy chapter of the Hounds of Hell lived here. The building had once been the home of the Mercy Sheriff's Department. It had plenty of rooms for members, meetings, and parties. Hell, the jail cells were still back there too. They sometimes came in handy.

Ryder had picked his brother up after he ditched the Cottonmouth bike he stole. Their plan to draw the rival MC out of Big Billy's had worked like a charm. "Have any trouble once I lost sight of you?" Hero asked them.

Axel laughed. "I left the bike at the Baptist church just outside of Mercy. They'll spot it easy enough."

"Did they spot *you*?" he asked.

The twins shook their heads in unison.

"You get the girl?" Ryder asked.

Hero tipped his head in the direction of his own room where he'd left her, sound asleep. Axel joined him at the table. Ryder grabbed glasses and a bottle of bourbon from the bar, pouring them each a drink. "She was drugged," Hero told them. "I walked right in after you led them off. I was going to be her first customer."

Ryder shook his head. "What the fuck?"

"What I want to know is why the hell they did this," Axel threw in. "It's not a huge secret Razor had a kid in town. That almost has to be the reason. The way Baby Face carved him up..."

"Is it?" Axel asked him. "And if they did take her because she's Razor's, why are *they* trying to start shit?"

They were valid questions. Hero didn't know the answers. "Maybe Razor knows." Hero took a drink of bourbon. "He just got out of surgery. Snow called. Said it was close, but it looks like he'll make it."

Axel nodded. "That's good news."

It was. According to Snow, Baby Face's blade had been an inch from causing significant damage to their president's insides. It was something that couldn't be ignored. It was too serious an offense. And somehow the stubborn son-of-a-bitch thought he was going to make an appearance at Mina Dock's funeral tomorrow.

"What happens now?" Ryder asked.

"We see how Razor wants to handle this," Hero told them. "He's the one Baby Face tried to gut."

"I don't know... I doubt Eli even knows about this," Ryder said. "Him and our dad grew up together. He's an asshole, but I can't see him ordering that kind of hit without a damn good reason."

"He wasn't the target," Hero pointed out. "She was." Hero just didn't know fucking why.

They sat drinking quietly, catching up on everything else. When it was almost midnight, the twins headed for their room. Hero went to his.

Razor's daughter was curled up on her side in his bed. She hadn't moved since he'd left her, and he did a double-take to make sure she was breathing. Carefully as he could, he pulled off her shoes and tucked her under the covers.

It still amazed him that his friend had a daughter who looked like *her*. Even as weak and strung out as she was, she was beautiful. Her face was all high cheekbones and soft curves, full lips. Her dark hair was wavy, spread out around her head like dark ribbons.

Hero had to wonder what she looked like smiling, all dressed up and feeling her best.

Probably the liquor talking. *Down boy.*

Handling her as he had back at Big Billy's had gotten him a little worked up. He wasn't proud of that.

They had spare rooms in the clubhouse, but he decided to stay right there. Just in case. The Cottonmouths had tried really hard to turn her out at Big Billy's. It wouldn't take them long to figure out who had intervened. He wasn't about to leave her alone and vulnerable. For Razor? Not entirely.

Stretching out on top of the bedding, Hero pulled off his boots and tried to sleep.

* * *

Jade

Jade woke up warm and comfortable. But she wasn't alone. Someone was spooned up behind her...

The events of the day before flooded her mind and she froze. When she slowly opened her eyes, she didn't recognize the room she was in. *Where was she now?*

A large hand slid up and down her upper arm, the gesture careful. "You okay?" a familiar voice asked. She remembered that deep voice. Her mouth and throat were dry. Probably from whatever they'd dosed her with. When she answered with "yes," it sounded more like a croak than a word.

Whoever he was, he moved behind her. He rolled away and then rolled back, a glass of water lowered into her field of vision. Somehow, she managed to get her hands on that glass, taking a couple of sips.

"Want to sit up?"

She nodded. Taking the water glass away, he

helped her ease onto her back and then to sit up. Propping pillows behind her, he looked her over as she leaned back on the pillows. "Where am I?" she asked him.

"Our clubhouse," he explained. "I'm Christian Hammond. They call me Hero."

She nodded. She would say so. He'd saved *her*. "I'm Jaeden Dock," she told him. "Did you say my father sent you to get me out of that place?"

Hero really was handsome. His hair was disheveled from sleep, and he scrubbed a hand through it to brush the longer waves away from his eyes. Now that she got a closer look at him, she realized his eyes were a bright sky blue.

"He did," he explained. "Well, he sent me to get you back. Sorry you ended up in *that* place."

"Me too."

His expression darkened as he studied her. "Did any of them... do anything to you before I got to you?"

It took her a moment to catch the real question he was asking. "They drugged me," she explained, still feeling it. "If anything else happened, I don't know."

Hero nodded. "We can have you looked at. We'll be going to the hospital a little later today."

By *we* did he mean she was going with him? Why the hospital?

"Did any of them tell you *why* they came after you?"

Jade tried to remember talking to the bikers who took her the first time she woke, what they said. "The main guy said everyone thought I was Razor's kid," she said slowly.

"Razor is Wade Gabriel."

That was the name Grams gave her over the years. Razor was her father then. "Then he said I was going to be a club slut… like my mother. I told them I was sorry. I didn't know her. She died when I was little. He was so angry. He told me that I was going to be sorry."

Hero tilted his head as he listened.

"He said they were taking me to that place so I could be a used-up whore." Jade fought the tears threatening to come on. "I'm not sure what I did."

"You didn't do anything wrong," he said after a moment, reaching out to cover one of her hands with his own. It was warm. "We need to figure out what their deal is."

Jade remembered something else that the one said. How close she'd come to being… "At one point, the main one asked the other two if they… wanted to break me in," she managed to say. "One of the others asked him if I was his half-sister."

He froze at that, considering what she'd just said. He ran a hand over his beard. "Huh. Do they think Eli was your father?"

"Who?"

"Eli is the president of the Cottonmouths," he explained. "Baby Face is his son."

"He's the one who grabbed me?"

Hero nodded.

"I'm so confused," she admitted, swiping at her tears with her free hand. Then another thought had her panicking. "I'm in town for my grandmother's funeral," she told him. "Has it…"

"The funeral is today," Hero told her.

"I need to be there." Her tone was filled with pleading, but she didn't care as long as she got to go. She needed to say goodbye.

"You'll get to go," he told her. "Everything starts at eleven, so we've got a couple of hours yet."

Jade let the tears come in her relief. She hadn't missed the funeral after all.

"We'll be going with you," he informed her. "Don't know why they're out to get you but they know you'll be there."

That thought had her anxiety gathering again. "Hero, where is my father?" she had to ask. "Why didn't *he* come for me?"

"He did," he said simply. "Baby Face took a knife to him. He spent several hours on the surgeon's table yesterday but he's going to make it. He wants to see you."

As nervous as she always thought she'd be to finally meet the man, it didn't seem like the scariest thing she had to deal with right now.

Did Hero mean that her father was injured trying to rescue her? There was so much she didn't understand. She wondered what time it was. Automatically, her hand went to her hip for her phone. Then she remembered Baby Face and his guys took it. "They have my phone," she told him.

Hero nodded.

"I've got to do something about that," she told him. "My friends will be worried and Emery…"

His hand tightened around hers. "We'll take care of it."

"My car?" Did they take that too? Was it where she left it?

Hero nodded. He'd been about to say something when someone started pounding on the door. "Yeah?" Hero called.

"Someone here to see the girl," a male voice called.

The next beat, the door flung open to reveal Emery who marched in, looking worried. "Jade," he said, rushing to the bed and grabbing her in a bear hug. "Thank God."

She was glad to see him too, hugging him back.

After a moment, Emery eased back to look at her. "What the hell happened? We've had people out looking for you." She didn't miss the glare he cut Hero.

"Baby Face and couple of his minions grabbed her off the street yesterday," Hero told him. "We got her back."

Emery narrowed his eyes at him. "Where's Razor?"

"Hospital," Hero told him. "Baby Face shanked him. He was in surgery for hours."

"You know what they could do to *her*?" Emery demanded.

A chill ran through her to think about what almost had happened.

Hero nodded, meeting the man's gaze.

"I'm going to take Jade back to the house so she can get ready for the funeral," Emery announced, rising from the bed. As he reached to help her to her feet, looking around for her shoes, Hero rose too. "We're going with you," Hero informed him.

Angry color flooded Emery's face. "The hell you are! I've been worried sick all night, praying nothing happened to Jade here. And if it weren't for you people, she wouldn't be in danger."

She placed a hand on her friend's forearm. "It's okay."

Emery didn't spare her a glance. "No, it's *not* okay."

While she had to admire him for standing up to the biker in her father's club, and he was half Hero's size, she needed to cut off a potential fight. She didn't want Emery to get hurt and honestly, she would feel better having Hero with her.

"They know I'm in town for the funeral," she told him. "If they show up for me there…"

Blowing out an exhale, Emery shook his head. "Fine. But once the funeral is over, you need to put moving back to Mercy out of your head. Mina, bless her soul, worked hard to keep you out of their cesspool all these years. You don't need to go jumping into it now."

Jade looked to Hero who appeared to be taking in everything they said. But she didn't know how to read him. After a moment, he motioned them toward the door. He was right behind them.

* * *

Jade had just finished dressing for the funeral. The rest of the morning after getting back to her grandmother's house had been a blur. Checking her look in the mirror, Jade realized she really didn't care how she looked. Sure, she'd know a lot of the people at the funeral. But she hadn't seen most of them in years. Grieving in front of the entire town wasn't something she felt ready to do. And she knew most of them would be there. Everyone had loved Mina Dock.

Jade had loved her so much. Tears stung the backs of her eyes as she realized that she was far from ready to say goodbye to the woman who taught her everything. The woman that nothing and no one in the world could stop. That was when she heard raised voices down below. *What was this?* Making her way down the stairs, the voices got louder.

"Mina didn't *want* him here," Emery's voice was loud. "She wouldn't have wanted *none* of you here. You understand?"

Hero filled much of the doorway, not permitting her grandmother's boyfriend entrance. Still, he sounded patient. "I understand that. We're just here to keep her safe. And we'll be doing that as long as she's here and until this gets resolved."

"Horseshit!" Emery yelled. "Wade's been beating that dead horse for a quarter century now. Jade shouldn't be in danger from anyone. She doesn't need none of you. So why don't you crawl back to your clubhouse and stay there. I'll have the cops keep an eye on things. Leave her alone!"

Jade didn't understand. She wasn't sure she wanted to. And she wasn't going to deal with it right now. "Emery?" she called, coming to a stop behind Hero.

Hero turned at the sound of her voice. He'd cleaned up, wearing a button-down shirt, a tie, and dark pants. She had to admit he looked very handsome. His gaze swept over her as he stepped back from the door.

The older man looked chagrined that she'd come upon the argument. He smiled weakly. "Are we ready to go?"

Nodding, she motioned him in. She didn't miss the frustrated exhale from Hero as he moved back to let Emery in the house. "Let me go get my things," she told them, not knowing how everything was going to go. She'd already agreed to let Emery go with her to the funeral. Would they make it through the ceremony without getting into a fight? Would Hero put up with him? Did it matter *what* he thought? What the hell was going on?

When she got back down to the door with her sweater and purse, Hero wasn't there. Emery seemed eager to talk with him out of earshot. "Jade, what were you thinking letting *him* in the house? Huh?" Emery's tone was a mix of frustration and worry. "None of them are any good. Don't you know that? If Mina had thought there was any good in any of them, do you think she would have kept them away from you?"

"Why *did* she keep me away?" Jade asked him. "From my father? Do you know?"

Emery's eyes were kind and sad. "That's a world you don't belong in. I don't care that he's your father. Mina didn't either. She did it to protect you."

"Okay, she didn't like bikers," Jade pointed out. "That was it? That was enough to justify to keeping a child away from her father? The only parent she had left?"

Now Emery looked uncomfortable. His gaze dropped. "Might have been more to it than that. I'm just... I'm sorry you never had that talk with her yourself. I think she planned to talk to you about it once you moved back..."

She saw his hands were shaking. "Emery?"

Tears had filled the old man's eyes. "I'm going to miss her so much."

"Me too." Jade wrapped her arms around him, and they stood there for a moment, in her grandmother's house.

When they walked out the door to Emery's pickup truck, she spotted a Jeep at the edge of the yard. Hero was driving and two men who looked like twins were in the back.

"They don't mean to follow us, do they?" Emery asked as he climbed in the cab of the truck.

Jade shrugged. "Everyone else will be there. Why not?" It was hard to keep a brave face when she considered what had happened yesterday. She was still tired, still groggy from the drugs. Her nerves were definitely on edge.

It was a quiet ride through the small Virginia

town to the church. Once Emery parked, Hero opened her door. He followed them closely as they walked in. Her grandmother had asked to be cremated and as she stood in front of the urn she'd take home with her, Jade fought back tears. *I miss you. How am I going to do this without you?*

Before long, Jade and Emery found a place to the side of the urn that held her grandmother's ashes and they greeted the people who came to pay their respects. Within moments, the entire church was filled with people. It didn't seem like the line would ever end. Jade grateful to have Emery by her side.

She was grateful for Hero and the twins too, particularly when an older man with white hair and a hard face wandered into the parlor. When his gaze met hers, her fear escalated, clawing inside her chest. Another biker dressed in his street clothes and his cut. The snake emblem looked less than pristine at the front of the man's cut, announcing he was a Cottonmouth. Her heart thundered in her chest.

In her peripheral vision, she watched Hero rise and head in her direction, standing right behind her now.

Who was he? She didn't have long to wait. When the mystery man reached the front, Emery shoved her behind him. Hero stepped in front of them both.

"The fuck you doin' here?" the mystery man asked.

The way he carried himself, the way Hero's spine straightened, told her whoever he was, he was someone important. Like Hero, he was tall and muscular. "Ask Razor," Hero told him.

The man sneered. "I ain't asking Razor shit." His dark-eyed gaze shifted to her. "You Vanessa's girl?"

Jade didn't know what to say so she nodded.

"I'll be seeing you," the man told Hero before strolling away, not in any hurry.

Jade was shaking as she watched him leave. She'd been so wrapped up in the confrontation, she didn't notice the next bikers in line until they stood in front of her, dressed like Hero. Again, Emery stepped in front of her.

"Emery," the new biker greeted before his gaze moved to her.

He was as tall as Hero but leaner. His handsome face was familiar, framed by long gun-metal gray hair that just touched his shoulders. Did she know him? Had she seen him before? He was older but she thought he might be the man from the picture with her mother.

Holding out a hand, he smiled. His hand shook slightly. He didn't look well. "Wade Gabriel."

Was this her father? She accepted his hand, shook it, despite Emery's obvious disapproval. "Jaeden Dock."

"I'm happy to meet you," he said, his voice rich and deep like good whiskey. "I'm very sorry about your grandmother… She was a fine woman."

Jade was blinking back tears. If the man *was* her father, it meant a lot for him to say that, considering Mina Dock had kept him away while she was alive. "Thank you," Jade said quietly.

"I'm sorry about what happened to *you*," he told her. "We'll talk later. I need to get my happy ass back to the hospital."

Hero looked concerned but shook his head at the man.

"Bring her to see me," Razor instructed. Nodding, he walked away. "Tomorrow."

Hadn't he just had surgery?

Once the line cleared, the minister walked up and motioned for them to have a seat so he could begin the service.

Chapter Four

Jade

The stream of people who came and went from the house until dark left Jade tired, resigned, and a little buzzed from drinking wine to numb the pain and calm her nerves. She was grateful for the well-wishes and offers of help. She also appreciated the sympathy casseroles that packed her grandmother's refrigerator and the old cooler she kept in the basement. She'd been in the fridge a couple of times to get more wine for herself or a drink for someone else, impressed by how everything was neatly packed in there.

Hero.

The gorgeous biker lingered in the kitchen and when he wasn't, which wasn't often, one of the twins was. But all the dishes were cleaned as they rolled in, and the kitchen looked just like Grams kept it. The only thing out of place was the ashtray at the center of the kitchen table and the haze of smoke that drifted out into the living room where Jade talked to her grandmother's friends and neighbors.

Grams would have had a fit about that.

When it got to eleven o'clock, Jade yawned as she listened to Emery and an old friend of his telling the story of a fishing trip her grandmother had gone on with them. Jade was embarrassed that she hadn't kept up with the storyline. All she could do was smile and nod when she thought she should, her eyes heavy and her sight blurry. They hurt because she couldn't recall how many times she'd cried that day between considering her loss and the caring words of others who loved Grams too. Fear that the other group of bikers would show up and start something preyed on her mind.

"Everyone?" Hero's deep voice called out in the living room. "Thank you for being here for Jade today. It's really appreciated. But she's going to fall asleep on you if she sits there much longer."

Norma Wilkins chuckled as she looked her over. "I think she's seeing two of me now." The kind lady with her white cloud of hair and warm smile carefully rose from Grams' platform rocker and stretched. Her hand was a warm press on Jade's forearm. "You rest. If you need anything, call me."

Jade thanked her, the Martins from down the street, and the woman who had once been Grams' teaching partner. Within ten minutes, the only one left was Emery, and he glared at Hero like a baleful cat.

Hero leaned against the wall at the entrance of the living room, his expression a challenge to the older man.

Emery shook his head from his spot next to her on the couch. "I still think it's a bad idea to have any of them stay in your house." Emery hooked a thumb in Hero's direction.

Blowing out an exhale, Jade rose to stand next to him. She didn't want to do this now and the fatigue on Emery's face told her he wasn't up for it either. "We'll talk about it tomorrow," she told him with a hug. "Be careful getting home."

"You get some sleep," he muttered close to her ear before grabbing his suit coat from the back of the chair and making his way to the front door. He turned back to shoot Hero a warning glance before he pushed open the screen door and made his way out into the warm spring night.

Pushing off from the wall, Hero grabbed a couple of plates and glasses left on the coffee table. His gaze on her was assessing, on two empty wine bottles in front of where she'd been sitting. "How are you holding up?"

Jade shrugged. "Honestly, I just want to go sleep for a week."

A corner of his mouth curled up. "You can if you want to."

Making her way up to her bedroom, she had no trouble falling asleep. But by two in the morning, she woke up, restless. In the T-shirt and sleep shorts she wore to bed, she tried to quietly make her way downstairs to the kitchen. Maybe a snack and some water would help her back to sleep.

The same creak on the second step from the bottom, the same old plastic magnets stuck to her Grams' fridge. Jade pulled the door to the fridge open. Packed with so many things, it looked ready to burst from the inside. Several cups of the cheap yogurt her grandmother always bought were shoved into a lower pocket in the door. It would do. Grabbing a blueberry cup and settling on a beer, she reached for the silverware drawer for a spoon.

The house was too quiet, too still. Grams had a certain energy about her. It made everyone around her, even the house, feel alive.

But she was gone now. And she was alone… Dropping the yogurt and beer on the counter, Jade tried to muffle her sobs in her hands, tried to get herself together in the shadows of the kitchen that was now hers. Mina Dock was gone. *Just gone.*

But the shadows of that mighty woman were all around her. The neatness and cleanliness of her house, the smell of the flowers from her garden. Quiet strength. Strength Jade didn't think she had.

"Hey," the deep voice had her jerking in surprise. She'd almost forgotten about her guest.

"I'm… sorry," she managed, trying to control her emotions but choking on them.

Strong arms wrapped around her, pulling her into his solid form. Jade surrendered to that strength and warmth, crying in the arms of a stranger. Strong hands smoothed up and down her back, his head gently leaning on hers. "I'm sorry." His voice was low, soft.

"She was… *alone*," she wailed through her tears. "I should have been here."

"You didn't know," he gently replied. "She wouldn't have told you."

Jade held him tighter, wrapping her arms around him. Her grandmother would never have let on that she was ill. She'd never admitted a weakness a day in her life.

"What am I going to do without her?" she wondered aloud. "I'm not like her… I never was."

"You'll survive," he whispered close to her ear. "You're not alone."

Her heart clenched in her chest at those words, wanting that to be true. She did have a handful of friends, but it wasn't the same as family. And her friends would be starting their lives too but in other places.

"You don't know him," Hero went on. "But your father? He's a good man. If he wasn't, I wouldn't be here. Give him a chance."

Burrowing into his chest, she felt those muscular arms tighten around her. She didn't want to give up that comfort yet. How long had it been since someone had held her?

"Come on."

She allowed him to steer her into the living room, to the couch. He let her get comfortable, still holding her. Pressing her ear to his bare chest, the strong sound of his heart was a comforting cadence in her ear. Trying to focus on it instead of the sting of loss, slowly she began to relax.

* * *

Jade didn't remember falling asleep on the couch. She was alone, one of her grandmother's throws draped over her to keep her warm. Opening her eyes when she heard footsteps, she watched Hero open the front door and grab items from the twins.

"Thanks, guys," he told them. "See you a little later." He paused, noticing she was awake. Hero stood in front of her with foam food boxes in hand and a duffel bag slung over his shoulder. One corner of his mouth curled up into a smirk. "Good morning, Jade."

She tried not to focus on the fact that she liked the way he said her name.

Moving past her, he headed for the kitchen. By the time she got up, wrapping the throw around herself, he was setting the boxes on the table before dropping his bag onto the floor.

"The guys got us sandwiches from the deli on Main Street," he explained as he began unpacking things. "Hope you're not one of those vegetarians."

He cocked an eyebrow at her, and it stopped her cold. *Damn, he's sexy.*

What had he said? "Oh, I tried it once," Jade admitted, her mind scrambling to catch up. "It didn't even last a semester."

Hero nodded, helping himself to her sink to rinse off his hands, then moving to the refrigerator. "What do we have to drink?"

"I've got beer," she offered. Yeah, it was her bougie IPA beer, but it was beer. She had to dig through all the food from friends to find it. If Hero minded when she set places for them at the table and placed one for each of them there, he didn't say. Jade took an appreciative bite of the corned beef sandwich he'd gotten her. "Thank you for this."

"No problem."

Tipping her head toward the bag he'd dropped on the kitchen floor, she asked, "What's that?"

"Overnight bag," he said simply. "The couch is fine."

What?

"Until we know what's going on with the Cottonmouths," Hero explained, "I'm your protection."

She wasn't sure what unnerved her more. Was it fear that the other biker gang would find a way to get her? Or was it the fact that the gorgeous biker she was having brunch with was staying with her in the house? "Do I get a say in this?" she asked.

Again, that smirk. "No, you don't."

"So you're just going to stay here until I head back to Providence?"

"About that," Hero said slowly, taking a drink of the beer and frowning as he looked at the label.

"What about it?" Jade pressed him. "You're not going *with* me, are you?"

"No." Those blue eyes swung up, his gaze meeting hers. "Your father is sending a crew to go pack everything up for you. They'll stop by tomorrow to talk to you about it."

She scoffed at that. "No," she said with a little fire. "That's… really not necessary."

Hero was staring her down. "It really is."

"And I don't know where my keys *are*," she realized. "Or my car."

Reaching into the pocket of his jeans, he pulled

out her keys and placed them on the table between them. "The guys brought your car. The keys were up in the visor. You do that?"

Jade nodded. She knew better than to leave keys in her car. She just did it when she was in a hurry. Then something else occurred to her. Putting the sandwich down, she shook her head. "And you're what? Just going to stay here with me until…"

"Until it's safe for me not to be here anymore," he said simply.

"What if it's months?"

"You've never talked to your father, have you?"

Are you kidding me? "No."

Hero chuckled. "It won't be months. But until this is settled, consider me your houseguest."

Jade wanted to play it cool, but she knew she missed that note by a mile. "What about my privacy?"

Hero took a bite of his sandwich, chewed slowly. She wondered for a moment if he'd even heard her. But he had, regarding her coolly. "You have a boyfriend or something?"

Jade didn't want to know what color she was turning. No, she didn't have a boyfriend. That wasn't the point. *Was he asking because he was interested?*

"I'll take that as a no," he said, before taking another swig of beer. "How do you drink this piss?"

"It's good beer," she told him. "Is this the type of houseguest you're going to be if I let you stay?"

Jade didn't like the look that earned her. "The good stuff costs less," Hero replied.

Losing patience, she finished her meal quickly. She went upstairs to collect her thoughts in the shower. Nothing had gone the way she thought it would on this trip. *Nothing.* She came to say goodbye to her Grams, to settle a few things. Then she was going back to Providence to pack up her things, release her apartment, and say goodbye to her friends. She had two weeks left on the lease, so she wasn't in a hurry.

Jade had made it to town, to Grams' house. *Her home.* And so far, she'd been warned about the bikers by her grandmother's boyfriend. She'd been kidnapped by one biker gang who tried to make her a prostitute. She'd been rescued by another biker who, along with her father's club, had decided that he'd be living on her couch until whatever elusive business involving her was settled.

She didn't even know what that fucking was. All she knew was that her father was the president of a motorcycle club called The Hounds of Hell. She'd never talked to him. She didn't know him.

Jade didn't want any part of this.

* * *

Hero

It was a warm spring day and since he'd already showered and dressed, Hero decided to wait out on her front porch while she got ready to go to the hospital. He'd already called Razor to tell him he'd be around in a couple of hours. Then he spied the garden off to the side of the house. Recently planted. Blowing out an exhale, Hero got up and wandered over. It needed to be watered. Weeded.

It didn't take him long to pull up the weeds. He'd just found the water hose attached to the side of the house when he heard the rumble of a bike draw near. Glancing over his shoulder, he saw a familiar figure park his ride at the edge of the lawn and pull off his helmet.

Eli Crizer headed straight for him with a determined pace. Dropping the hose next to the garden, Hero walked up to meet him. *This ought to be good.* "Eli," Hero greeted him.

"Hero, I'm hearing some pretty wild fucking stories this morning," Eli said flatly. "Hoping you can help me make sense of it."

"Be glad to."

"Was a couple of your guys over at Big Billy's night before last?" the Cottonmouth president asked.

"Why?"

Eli's eyes narrowed on him. "Well, I hear tell that someone stole one of our member's bikes, did donuts in the lot to get everyone's attention. Then whoever this fella was, he led them on a merry chase."

"Huh." Hero shrugged. "Did you find the bike?"

"Not yet," Eli told him. "On top of that, someone made off with one of our girls from the club. Just carried her right out. Another girl described a fellow that sounds an awful lot like *you*."

Hero's jaw locked and he stared the other man down. "Who was the girl they took?"

Angry color seeped up from Eli's collar, making the snake tattoo that ran up his neck appear darker, menacing. "Does it matter?" Eli asked angrily.

"It does," Hero shot back. "Your club in the habit of kidnapping women and forcing them to work on their back?"

The confusion edging the other man's expression told Hero something wasn't right. "What the hell are you talking about?"

"They kidnapped that girl off the street," Hero explained. "They drugged her and took her off to Big Billy's. She's not a club slut and she wasn't there of her own free will."

"You're making some serious charges, Hero." Eli's tone held a warning.

"I am." Hero held the other man's gaze.

"I haven't even told you the best part," Eli went on. "Three of my guys are missing. I'm wondering if anything happened to them."

Hero inched closer, barely keeping control of his temper. "We'd like a word with them too," Hero told him.

"Come again?" Eli's tone held a note of warning.

"You heard me," Hero told him. "Baby Face, Big Dog, and Jimmy Jazz. I watched the three of them toss her into the back of a white van and drive off. There was a driver too, but I didn't get a look at him."

Eli held his ground. "You were there?"

Hero nodded. "We followed them down to the Reid place and tried to cut them off before they could drive off with her again. We had a confrontation."

That had Eli's interest. "Did you now?"

"I shot Big Dog in the jaw." Hero had nothing to hide. "Baby Face gutted Razor like a fish. Razor spent hours on the surgeon's table and he's going to make it. But it was close."

The grave expression on Eli's face was telling. "And the girl? Where did you take her?"

Hero held his hands out, motioning the yard around them, the house it surrounded. Hero knew the second Eli realized who they were talking about.

"Son of a bitch," he muttered under his breath. "Mina Dock's granddaughter."

"The same."

"And you just happened to be there?" Eli asked, his expression skeptical.

"No, Razor sent me to watch over her."

"If what you say really happened, sounds like you did a shit job." Eli chuckled. "Razor…"

"He's going to want to talk to you." Hero didn't

need to tell him. He hooked his thumb in the direction of the house. "Any idea why your son is interested in her?"

"I might have an idea or two." Eli didn't look happy. "When Razor's up to it, I'll meet with him."

"And Baby Face?" Hero asked.

"Leave him to me," Eli told him.

"You know we can't do that."

"We'll see." Eli turned to head back to his bike. "Tell me when the meeting with Razor's set."

"Will do." After a moment, Hero added, "Check the old Baptist church lot."

Eli stopped and shot him a look over his shoulder. Hero watched him return to his bike, ride off.

Turning back to fish the water hose out of the yard, he looked up to see Jade standing in an upstairs window, watching in alarm. Until they figured things out, Baby Face was a threat to her. The sadistic little bastard wasn't getting anywhere near her. Not again.

Chapter Five

Jade

Jade regretted wearing the summer dress the minute they stepped into the hospital. It was so cold.

She followed Hero into Mercy hospital, down several corridors until they reached a room near the end of the hall. Inside was a lone hospital bed with her father in it. He was hooked up to all manner of machines, looking a little better than he had yesterday when he had managed to come to the church for Mina's funeral. Still, she hoped he was going to be okay as her gaze moved over him.

"I look bad, huh?" Her father scrubbed a hand through his hair, sweeping the shiny metal-colored locks away from his face. "Hey, there," he said in that deep whiskey voice. "Thanks for coming, Jade."

She nodded, smiled. Hero grabbed one of the stuffed chairs and dragged it close to the bed before taking a seat. "How are you feeling?" she asked, coming to sit next to him on the bed, putting herself between the two men.

The charming smile slipped from his face as his gaze moved over her. The emotion in his hazel eyes had her heart squeezing in her chest. "You look just like Vanessa," he said after a moment.

"Grams told me that a lot."

Razor nodded. "How are *you* doing?"

Jade knew what he was really asking. "I'm… I'm fine. I'm just… I'm sorry this happened to *you*. If I did anything…"

"Hey, no." Razor covered one of her hands with his. "You didn't do anything wrong. What happened to me wasn't your fault. I had a bad feeling something was going on when word got out that Mina died.

People started asking about you. I should have done more."

"How much trouble did you get into for escaping yesterday?" Hero asked him.

Razor's grin was back. "I got read the riot act."

Hero laughed at that.

Her father's gaze turned speculative. "It was worth it. I needed to pay my respects."

To a woman who never let him see his daughter. That only created more questions in her head.

"What happened?" Razor asked carefully.

She explained getting into town, her discussion with Emery. Then she mentioned she'd driven into Mercy for something to eat. And that's when they'd grabbed her, drugging her. The tears threatened again as she described waking up, the confrontation. "That main guy... Baby Face? Oh, God. It was like... he hated me. He hated me so much," she explained. Tears began to sting the back of her eyes.

"Jade," Hero said softly. "Tell him what he said to you."

Taking a deep breath, Jade told him. "Baby Face told me I would be sorry. He said I'd be a used-up whore like my mother." When she got to the last part, she hesitated, feeling fragile now that she was facing her father. The man she'd never been allowed to see most of her life.

"The bastard suggested that him and Big Dog and Jimmy Jazz should break her in," Hero said when she couldn't. "Then one of them asked Baby Face if she wasn't *his* half-sister? You know what he meant by that?"

Razor's gaze moved from Hero to her. It seemed like he was trying to figure out what to say. His fingers tightened around hers. "Honey, Vanessa, your mother, wasn't a whore," Razor explained carefully. "A wild child? Maybe. But she didn't make the rounds. She wasn't hooking up with any biker she could find trying to be someone's old lady. She only had two other boyfriends before me."

And to hear her grandmother tell it, no one after Razor. She could feel Hero's gaze on her. "Eli?" he asked.

"He was one," Razor muttered, his gaze staying on her.

Her confusion must have shown on her face. "My Mom dated Eli? Baby Face was his son, and he thinks I am his half-sister? Does Eli think that too?"

Her father studied her speculatively. "Maybe so."

She didn't want to ask the question. Just thinking it had her heart racing. "Do we really know who's my father?" Somehow, she got the words out.

Razor didn't appear surprised. He sighed. "I offered to do a paternity test," he finally said. "So many times. Your grandmother wouldn't hear of it. And Eli never darkened their doorstep to my knowledge."

Oh, she could see Grams in her mind's eye, telling her to run in the house when Razor showed up.

"I'd be glad to do one now if you need that. But honestly, there's no doubt in my mind who you are. You *are* my kid."

"My Mom was pregnant before me," she told him, tears pooling in her eyes at his honesty and conviction.

"What I heard," he replied. "Rumor had it that the father was a Cottonmouth. Vanessa told me she lost it. That was some weeks before she ever gave *me* the time of day."

Swiping at her tears with her free hand, Jade decided to tuck that away to consider later. "Why was I never allowed to see you?" Jade finally asked the question that had haunted her most of her life. "Grams always said we'd have that talk but we never did. I just…"

Something in the older man's expression softened. "Mina was a good woman, looking after her family. I don't blame her for the decisions she made. Didn't stop me from trying to change her mind. Sometimes I wasn't exactly nice about it." His gaze cut to Hero and back to her. "She ever tell you much about your grandfather? Vanessa's father?"

Jade shook her head. "He died when my mom was a kid. But she didn't talk about him much. I didn't get the impression their relationship was a happy one."

Razor's smirk confirmed it. "It wasn't. Mostly because he was one of us."

"What?" She hadn't expected that. "He was…"

"A Hound, and good friends with *my* father," Razor offered. "Now, Mina knew that going in. She still married him. But she never could square with the club. She never accepted it, didn't want our help. But anything that went wrong was the club's fault."

Jade hadn't known that. All she knew of her grandfather were a couple of small, framed photographs. He hadn't *looked* like a biker in those. "What happened to him?" instinct had her asking.

"I was a prospect back then," Razor explained. "He took a couple of guys to deliver guns to a client. We hadn't done business with that group before. Things went very wrong. Your grandfather ended up with a bullet in the head. All four of them that went? Dead."

Jade's heart sank to consider that loss. Her

grandmother's actions where she was concerned were starting to make sense.

"Mina tried hard to keep Vanessa away from it all," Razor explained. "But it seemed like the more she did, the more Vanessa defied her. She started finding her way into clubs and parties just out of high school."

Her mother's history was another subject Grams discussed sparingly. She'd tell Jade about her mother growing up, the things she liked and liked to do. Never did she talk about her mother's time with the MCs.

Razor sighed. "She actually didn't start up with the Hounds until later. She was sweet on a boy who was a prospect for the Cottonmouths first. She was in that club for a couple of years. That guy was her first love. He ended up moving to Alabama, signing on with a chapter down there. He left her behind."

Jade nodded, listening.

"Now, I'm told she found herself in a family way during that time," Razor went on. "Guess I always thought that younger guy was the father but now I'm wondering… Was it Eli? I don't know."

She looked to Hero and back to Razor. Her mother lost the pregnancy because of alcohol and drug use. At least, that's what Grams told her.

"Eli was the one that came to the house earlier," Hero explained. "He's the president of the Cottonmouths."

That got Razor's attention. "Did he?"

Hero nodded.

Jade could tell from the look exchanged between the two men that there would be a discussion about that later. Razor turned his attention back to her. She appreciated someone finally trying to answer her questions about the past.

"Vanessa lost that child," Razor stated.

She nodded. That story matched what Grams told her.

"Mina got your mother into rehab, tried to get her clean," he went on. "It didn't last. Around that time, she started showing up at our parties. I'd just become an official member of the Hounds and she was like me, looking for a good time."

Jade didn't know what to take away from that.

"But I screwed up," Razor admitted. "I fell for her."

The look on his face told her he meant that. He'd cared about her mother... That had her thinking. "How much time was between the first pregnancy and..."

A quick glance over her shoulder showed her that Hero was interested in that answer too. Razor's gaze dropped. "Not enough."

Hero's brows went up.

"I get why anyone might think you were Eli's but... no. That's not the truth," he said sadly.

"So when she told you... about me..." She hated the sad note in her own voice.

"I was young and dumb," Razor admitted. "When she told me, I panicked. I acted badly."

That explains a lot.

"Not a day goes by that I don't regret that," Razor said meaningfully. "Instead of looking at the promise I had right before me, I was feeling sorry for myself. I was worried about my standing in the club. *My* future."

Jade thought about what Grams had gone through with her husband. By the time her mother got into the MCs, alcohol and drugs, and then the pregnancies? She understood now why Grams had done what she had.

"I should have asked her to be my old lady

then," Razor told her. "By the time my dumb ass realized what needed to happen, Mina had her under lock and key. She said she'd meet me once when I got a message to her, but she didn't show. Then she died."

But her father had never stopped trying to see her. Her heart cracked in her chest to think about it. "Did you ever find anyone else?" she asked quietly.

"No…" he said slowly. "I don't expect anything from you. But I'd be grateful to get to know you. On your terms."

Jade nodded, carefully hugged him. Her heart was thumping so loudly both men could probably hear it. Her father wanted to have a relationship with her. Should she give him a chance? "I'd like that too. When Grams passed, she left me her house. I was thinking about moving back home. But now, I don't know." She didn't miss the silent communication between the two men.

"Think about it," Razor told her. "You don't have to decide anything right now. But I'll support you, whatever you decide to do."

"Thank you for telling me," she said. She meant it.

* * *

Hero drove them back to her house in his Jeep, just stopping for gas and "good beer." Talking with her father had left her quite a bit to think about and Hero seemed to understand that, giving her a cold one for the ride home without saying anything. The silence was comfortable in the SUV as they pulled up in the driveway.

"Thank you for the garden," she told him as he put the vehicle in park.

"You're welcome," he told her, his blue-eyed gaze on her as he shut the engine off. When he hesitated, her attention was on him. "You told Razor that you were rethinking moving down here."

Jade nodded. "Do you blame me?"

"No." Hero's hands dropped to his lap. "I'm hoping you'll rethink that again."

Her heart sped up at that. It shouldn't, but it did. The last thing she needed was another failed relationship, even with someone who looked as good as he did. Sure, he was gorgeous. She'd loved falling asleep in his arms. She wasn't at all ready to admit it though. "Wouldn't I be safer back in Providence?" she asked.

"Not if Baby Face decided to follow you there. Until we know what his motives are, you're safer here with us."

Hero might be right. And Jade had planned to move into her childhood home. Truth be told, she didn't like having her choices taken away. On one level, she got that it wasn't her father's fault nor Hero's. But it was still a sticking point with her. She sighed. "Look, I have two weeks left on my lease back in Providence," she explained. "Either way, I've got to go back and grab my things. And I've been giving that some thought, Hero... I'm going to take care of that myself. I appreciate the offer of help but..."

Nodding, he opened the door of the Jeep and climbed out, grabbing the bag of beer as he did. She got out and followed him to the door, unlocking it to let them in. When Hero didn't answer, she followed him into the kitchen. "Did you hear me?"

"I did," he said, pulling the beer in their carton from the bag and placing them on the counter. He handed her another one -- the bottle in her hand was empty -- before leaning against the counter in front of the kitchen sink with his, twisting off the cap.

"So that's settled?" She opened her second beer.

After a minute, he shook his head. "Hardly."

"What do you mean, *hardly*?"

"It would be safest if you stayed here and let us go take care of everything." Hero's tone was firm. "The twins are good guys. They aren't going to tear your shit up or take anything if that's what you're worried about."

Shaking her head, Jade scoffed. "I don't know them so yeah, that's a concern. But that's not the problem. The problem is I have almost two weeks left on that lease. That gives me time to go up there, take my time packing up things. I can settle my affairs and say goodbye to my friends. That was what I *planned* to do."

Hero shrugged a shoulder, taking a drink. "Sorry to disrupt your plans."

Almost since she arrived in town, Jade had been anxious. Hero had been her shadow since she arrived. Gorgeous as he was, she didn't like feeling like her life was out of her control. She worked on the beer, feeling his gaze on her. She hadn't eaten much, and the alcohol went to her head. Yeah, she'd been drinking too much but she needed it to numb her out and give her respite.

"*Why* are you disrupting my plans?" Frustration bled into her voice. "I appreciate your help in getting me out of there. I really do. But since then, you've been here. You're moving in and planning to send your buddies to clear my apartment. I'd really just like to have a say in how my own life goes."

"I get that," Hero said after a moment. "But right now, I need you to trust me."

Jade was tired and still having questions in her head wasn't helping at all. "What if Emery is right? Maybe me being part of your world is a mistake." Her mind conjured up her father. "Grams never allowed me to meet my father while she was alive. I understand why now. She had a good reason, and I had no trouble until I came back here."

"You act like it's a choice you can make." Hero leaned back against the sink with his arms crossed over his muscular chest. "It's not a choice. Like it or not, you *are* part of all this."

Her mind spun. Yeah, she was tired and stressed. She'd had a little bit to drink. But the more she tried to discuss what she needed to do in the immediate future with Hero, the more frustrated she became when he told her there were other plans. Grams had just passed away. The house was now hers. She needed to decide if she was going to stay here or return to Providence. Why was she letting a bunch of bikers tell her how it was going to be? Especially when her life had been upended because of them at the worst possible time. She'd been snatched off the street and drugged. Maybe what she needed was to get to the police.

And on that note, she headed up the stairs for her bedroom. Somehow, she'd managed to put away her second beer in short order. It wasn't the best idea considering she planned to go to the sheriff's department, but it helped her keep her fears at bay.

It was impressive really. In fifteen minutes flat, she'd changed into jeans with a tank top and sneakers. She had her purse, her keys. She was going to do this. She was going to get the law involved. Emery would be happy.

Biker twins be damned. Creeping down the stairs, she didn't see Hero in the kitchen. He wasn't in the living room either. *Good.* Maybe he left for the evening. She didn't give a damn. She had a plan, and she was going to see it through. Sure, it was messed up to show up in the state she was in, inebriated and emotionally wrecked, but maybe they'd understand.

Jade locked the house up and headed for her vehicle. Hero came around the other side of the SUV, dropping a shoulder and slinging her over it while she fought the lurch in her stomach the movement caused. Her purse dropped into the grass.

By the time he'd scooped up her purse, climbed back up to the front door, and plucked the keys out of her hand, she was beating the hell out of his back with tight fists, trying not to throw up because being carried like a potato sack wasn't doing her inebriated self any favors. "Put me down!"

Hero carried her back into her house, dropping her unceremoniously on the couch. It took Jade a moment for her head to stop spinning. Then she was curling up, trying to roll off to the side. Hero stood above her, looking ready to cut her off.

"Move!"

Hero shook his head, watching her intently. "Where do you think you're going?"

"Sheriff's department."

"That's not happening," he said tersely. "Let me and Razor handle this."

"No." She managed to get on her feet to stand clumsily. "This is what needs to happen. I don't give a shit what you or my father want."

"You're not getting behind the wheel in the state you're in," he warned.

Jade glared at her handsome, if uninvited, houseguest. "Watch me."

She made it maybe a foot when a long, powerful arm wrapped around her upper body like a band of steel. Pulling her back into his body, Hero held her there while she twisted and kicked, fighting to escape his clutches.

It didn't take her long to realize he was letting her tire herself out. Jade played along. When her efforts slowed down, his hold on her loosened ever so slightly. But when she tried to get away, she couldn't.

The tears came then. Yes, there were tears for her loss. Grams had been the world to her. But there were also tears of anger and frustration. Maybe Emery had a point. Handsome as the biker bastard that held her was, he'd still come into her life and taken control. What gave him the right? She needed to take that control back. Somehow in her alcohol-addled brain, doing battle with the gorgeous biker seemed like a good idea.

"Are you done?" Hero asked. That he sounded tired now was satisfying.

Ceasing her resistance, Jade panted, struggling to breathe. "What else?" she demanded, ducking out of his hold and spinning to confront him. "What else am I *not* allowed to do?"

Hero didn't like that question. She could tell. "Anything that risks you falling into the hands of the Cottonmouths," he said finally.

It was easy to recall her fear at being taken by the other crazy bikers. No, she didn't want to take that risk. Still... Jade threw her hands up. "Why are they doing this? I haven't done anything to them that I'm aware of. What the fuck do they want with me?"

Hero's hands went to his hips, his gaze speculative. "Doesn't matter what they want with you."

"The hell it doesn't," she told him. "Grams left me this house. I grew up here. I deserve to be able to live here if I want. Or go back to Providence. Either way, I deserve to feel safe."

"Not arguing that."

"Whatever the Cottonmouths' problem with me is," Jade swiped at her tears, "isn't my problem. I'm not going to live the rest of my life afraid of them. It's not fair."

With a deep sigh, Hero took a step closer.

"How long is this supposed to go on?" she whined, hating the sound of herself. More, she hated the spiral of fears in her head. "Are they going to kill me? Are they…"

"Hey," Hero pulled her against him, his arms strong and warm.

Jade sank into that warmth even while the restlessness and frustration remained. She still wanted to run away from this. She still wanted to demand answers from Hero, from anybody who could tell her what the fuck was going on.

Hero's heart pounded in a strong, steady cadence beneath her ear. "I don't know why the Cottonmouths want you." His voice was low. "Our clubs have always had bad blood between them. Razor and Eli hate each other. It's not exactly a secret that you're Razor's kid."

Wrapped up in his arms, her heart was flying. "Razor asked you take care of me?"

"He sent me to keep an eye on you when you got into town," he admitted.

"And now?"

"I'm here because I want to be."

Jade gazed up at him, not hesitating when his mouth claimed hers. His lips caressed hers, softly at first. She let him pull her closer, let him deepen the kiss. Sliding her hands up around his neck, she got her fingers into the cool silk of his hair.

Hero felt so solid and strong against her, her heart beating next to his as their lips danced together.

He tasted of the beer they'd drunk, of longing. His hands smoothed over her back in enticing circles, sending ripples of pleasure through the rest of her. The press of his heated length against her had her thighs clenching, had her wanting more.

Hero steered them toward the couch, but Jade broke the kiss, shaking her head. The big windows there in the living room were barely framed by frilly curtains.

"Not here," she muttered, motioning toward the stairs.

Hero wasted no time in scooping her up bridal style and hustling up the stairs with a speed that was impressive.

Her back met the firm mattress of her bed. Hero was on her a beat later, his hands in her hair, his mouth demanding on hers. Grabbing his leather cut, she worked at pushing it off his shoulders and he helped her. She was already hauling up his T-shirt, wanting to see him, as he shrugged off the cut.

It was worth the effort. Hero was all muscle under there with a sprinkling of hair a shade darker than what was on his head. Tattoos littered his chest and arms as his upper body was revealed. The sight pushed up her excitement. Jade had only ever dated vanilla, nerdy types who didn't have tats or defined abs like he did. *Hot damn.*

The cocky smirk was back as her hands roamed greedily over his chest and arms, letting her take it all in. But his patience didn't last. Hero came for her, dropping onto his forearms and burning her down with a kiss that curled her toes.

When she went for the front of his jeans, he stopped her. "Nope. Your turn."

She didn't fight him when he whipped the tank

top up and off her. The elastic of her bra snapped against her skin as he got rid of it just as quickly. When he got his hands and mouth on her breasts, it took her breath away. Jade's hands were clutched in his hair as his lips spread around one of her nipples. The wet lash of his tongue on the tight peak had her writhing beneath him.

When his lips returned to hers, he kissed her breathless as his hands worked the front of her jeans. "Jade, you're beautiful," he murmured, pulling the jeans open and peeling them and her panties off. "So soft and beautiful."

"Hero…"

He had her completely bared to him in seconds, wasting no time in dropping more kisses over her breasts, down to her tummy. Jade was so worked up that her body was weeping for him.

He hummed against her skin as he made room for himself between her thighs. She felt that deep sound in her pussy. Wrapping those strong arms around her thighs, he held her open to get his mouth on her. He had her dancing mindlessly on the tip of his tongue in seconds, holding her hips down and drowning her in her own rising pleasure.

Jade pawed at the bedding, his shoulders, and head as he took her apart. When he worked a finger into her aching channel, she struggled to breathe. When he added a second, curling them just so against her hidden trigger, she went wild beneath him. Her cries filled the room as he held her there, drawing out her release until the room spun around her.

When she was dazed and panting beneath him, he lifted from her to undo his jeans, to push them down his slim hips. He wore nothing beneath them, and the swollen stalk of his cock greeted her. Oh, she wanted *that*.

Taking himself in hand, he stroked his cock as his heated gaze roamed her. When she reached for him, he let her take over. The velvety length of him felt so good.

"You on the pill?" he asked, his breath coming as fast as hers.

Jade nodded. She'd never been so grateful for that protection in her life.

"Thank fuck," he muttered, dropping over her and lining himself up at her entrance.

When he began pushing into her, it stung. It had been a while for her. But she wrapped her arms and legs around him, holding on as her body stretched around his cock. Her wetness eased his way until he was buried inside her as far as he could go, hard and throbbing.

Hero felt so good in her arms, her fingers digging into the muscles of his back. He gave her a moment to adjust, blazing a trail over her neck with heated lips. Jade pumped her hips beneath him, ready to go.

It was all the provocation he needed. Hero's thrusts started slow and easy, dazzling her with his size and the fact that he was hitting pleasure points inside her that she never knew she had. Her body clenched around him as he loved her, her nails digging into his skin.

"You feel so damn good, baby," Hero huffed into her ear. "So good."

Jade moved with him, trying to keep up. When his lips found hers again, she kissed him back for all she worth. His thrusts came faster and harder, causing a new wave of pleasure to swell inside her. "You're going to come so hard, aren't you?" he whispered against her lips.

Jade wasn't capable of speech. When he changed the angle of his thrusts, he hit just the right spot. Her cries filled the room as he nailed that spot, again and again, until she came hard around him, hanging on to him like a life raft in a storm.

Hero was chasing his own release then, his hold on her tightening. She knew the minute he'd reached it, his thrusts punching the air from her lungs as a cry escaped him. Pulling himself out at the last minute, thick white ropes of his release streaked her thighs as he worked himself.

Her eyes slid closed. The fabric of his T-shirt was soft when he used it to clean her off. Then he rolled on to his back, carefully pulling her with him until she draped over him, sweaty and breathless as he was. Jade smiled up at him. "Is that why you want me to stay here?"

Hero's eyes were closed but he was smiling. "Yeah."

His heartbeat was strong against her palm. "Think my father will be mad?"

He bounced her on his chest, and he chuckled. "Probably. But it's an ass beating I'm willing to take."

"For the sex?" she couldn't help asking.

"For *you*," he said quietly. "Sex is just part of it."

Her heart skipped a beat at those words.

Chapter Six

Hero

The hum of his phone woke him up. Spooned up behind Jade, Hero scrambled on the bed to reach his jeans. He had his phone in hand by the third hum. It was eleven at night.

It was Snow. "Hero?"

"Yeah."

"Where are you?" Snow asked, talking and music in the background.

"At Jade's place." At least he was hoping she'd keep it. "Mina Dock's house." Pulling his jeans on, Hero held his phone to his ear with his shoulder. "What's up?" A quick glance at the bed showed him Jade was still sound asleep, snuggled into the center of the bed. She needed the rest.

"I'm at Sackett's," Snow told him.

Emery Phillips' bar? "Yeah?" Hero prompted him, walking quietly out of the bedroom.

"Yeah. Mackenzie Rigby is here."

Was Snow drunk? Why was he calling him about a woman at the bar? "And?"

"And she told me a story," Snow went on. "Hang on."

The background noise was faded, the sound of Snow walking told him his fellow Hound was making his way outside. "Yeah. Mackenzie says hi by the way."

Hero bet she did. The girl had been a club slut for the Cottonmouths for years before she defected, started hanging out at Hound joints. She'd been with Baby Face for a time, had his signature slice on her jaw for her efforts. The bastard loved marking up girls.

"Anyway, she still has a few ties to the

Cottonmouths, right? She heard through the grapevine that Baby Face has found himself with a shit ton of gambling debt. He's got goons out looking for him, just like we are."

That stopped Hero on the stairs. "Really?"

"Really."

The thought of letting it ride and letting the loan sharks get him was tempting. But impossible. Baby Face had knifed Razor and that had to be dealt with. The MC's reputation demanded it. Besides, until this was dealt with, the little fucker was a threat to Jade. Hero wasn't having that.

"Does Eli know?" Hero made it to the bottom of the stairs, heading into the kitchen.

"That's just it," Snow explained. "I would think so."

Hero was tired, his brain wasn't up to full speed yet. "You think this has something to do with Razor's daughter?"

"I do. Eli's apparently worth some money. Couldn't Baby Face be trying to get rid of her? Especially if he thinks she's Eli's kid?"

Hero pulled another beer out of the fridge, twisted off the top. "How would that help him?" Hero wasn't following. "If he needs money so bad, can't he get it from Eli?"

"Mackenzie got the impression that it's a very sore subject for Eli. Guess he already tried that route."

"What's that got to do with Jade?" Hero asked.

"That's the part I'm wondering about, Hero," his friend went on. "I'm thinking he either handed her off to Billy for money to put on his debt or…"

"Or?" Hero's temper flared.

"Or he's planning to move against Eli, and he doesn't want to compete with her if there is any chance she's Eli's kid and not Razor's."

"Fuck." It was plausible. Hell, Baby Face could be killing two birds with one stone. "Anyone seen Baby Face?"

"Nothing," Snow told him. "I'll let you know if I can find out anything else."

"Thank you." Swearing under his breath, Hero ended the call.

Money trouble made people do fucked up things. If Baby Face had a lot of gambling debt and Eli wasn't willing to help him? Yeah, it made sense that he tried to sell Jade. If he decided to move against Eli to get the money that way, he wouldn't want Jade to be able to make a claim to his estate. Or his plan could include doing both. *Fuck.*

Hero wasn't about to let anything happen to Jade. And not just because she was Razor's kid. He didn't give a damn who her father was. Hero was keeping her. But their situation was fragile. No one seemed to know where Baby Face and his friends were, and they were after *her.* He'd attacked their prez who was now in the hospital. That wasn't good. It could give the impression that their MC was leaderless, weak.

"Hero?"

He never heard her come down the stairs, looking sleepy and adorable. She'd dressed but her feet were bare, her dark hair pulled back into a ponytail. It was easy to read the worry in her expression.

"Who was that?" she asked.

"Snow," he explained. "You'll meet him soon. He's our VP."

Nodding, she padded past him to sink into one of the kitchen chairs. "Is everything okay?" she asked him.

Taking a knee by her chair, he stretched up to kiss her mouth. He smoothed her hair back from her pretty face. "We might have some idea of what's going on with Baby Face," he explained. "Money problems. And money makes people do desperate things."

Jade looked more awake then. He didn't miss the slight tremble of her hands in her lap. He covered them with his own.

"I need you to understand that going to the cops or Providence right now is a bad idea," he said carefully, needing her to listen. "In fact, I'm thinking that maybe we should stay at the clubhouse. We'd stand a better chance there than we would if they came at us here." He watched her throat work as she swallowed nervously.

"But the house? What if they…"

He brushed a kiss on her forehead. "Honey, I know this house means a lot to you. But *you* matter more. We can have the prospects keep an eye on it for us. How about that?"

She didn't look convinced but after a moment, she nodded. "Maybe you're right. Now that I can think about everything a little more clearly. Maybe that would be best."

"Yeah?" he asked. "Why don't you head up and throw some things together you need? I'd like to get over there as soon as we can, okay?"

Hero rose then but she didn't follow suit.

"Will they go after Emery?" she thought to ask.

He loved that his girl had a big heart. Hero shook his head. "Emery is too visible. Most MCs in this area go to his place, at least once in a while. Baby Face can't take that risk even if he is fucking desperate."

Her gaze dropped, she nodded. Quiet as a mouse, she stood, turned and headed back for the stairs while he watched.

It was a shit time to be going through what she was. It added insult to injury considering she was here because of Mina Dock's passing. It steeled his resolve to keep her safe and get retribution for her father.

* * *

Razor

A tap at the door pulled Razor out of his nap. He expected to see one of the nurses who'd been helping him, or maybe one of his guys. What he didn't expect was Eli, president of the Cottonmouths. The man he'd known for years made his way into Razor's hospital room, his gaze sweeping over Razor as he approached the bed.

"Well, you look like a mile of hammered shit," Eli told him.

"Feel like it too," Razor admitted.

Either Snow or Hero must have talked to Eli, told him what happened. Razor's gaze locked with the other man's, letting him take the lead for now. He watched as Eli grabbed one of the chairs, pulling it closer to his bedside.

"My boy did this?" Eli nodded to his midsection.

"He did." Razor had known Eli for a long time. He was a smug son of a bitch when he wanted to take credit for something. Just now, Razor didn't get that impression. "You authorize this?"

That earned him a look. "You know I didn't," Eli told him. "If I'd had a problem with you, I wouldn't have sent my kid. I would have come myself."

Razor didn't argue the point. "I wasn't the problem for him," Razor said. "My girl was. Know anything about that?"

Eli held his gaze but seemed to be considering

what he'd say. That was new. Eli was famous for being a hot head. It was one quality Baby Face had inherited. That Eli was hesitant and careful? It spoke volumes. "Mina Dock's granddaughter, right? Vanessa's girl?"

"That's the one," Razor replied.

"And you're sure *you're* her father?"

"Haven't gotten around to doing a paternity test yet," Razor explained. "She just got into town a couple of days ago and I've been laid up here about that long." When Eli didn't have an answer, Razor studied him. "Why are you asking, Eli?"

"Because Vanessa was seeing me before that girl was born."

Razor nodded. He was aware. "Vanessa lost a pregnancy before my girl was born," Razor told him.

Eli shifted in the chair, scrubbing a hand over his beard in what looked like agitation. "I was with her after she lost that pregnancy," Eli told him, a muscle twitching at his jaw. "There is a good chance that the girl is mine."

I don't think so. Razor blew out an exhale, shifting in his bed and hoping it was almost time for his pain meds. Muscling his way past the discomfort, he considered the big picture. "We'll have to sort that out later," Razor told him. "Right now, your boy is out there, and he's after my girl. He meant fucking business. He ripped me open, Eli. Have an idea why?"

At that, Eli's gaze dropped, and he hung his head.

Oh, he has an idea all right. It startled Razor a little when Eli rose to start pacing by the chair. "I told his dumb ass to give up gambling," Eli told him, scrubbing a hand through his hair. "The more I scotched for him, the more he expected. I had to quit bailing him out. When I did, he got real fucking quiet about it."

Razor bet he did.

"And now he does this shit," Eli went on. "You of all people know how bad this fucking looks for our club."

Razor did. But that was the least of his worries right now. "Eli, I'm more concerned by him selling my girl for Big Billy to turn out." Razor stared him down and after a beat the other man stopped pacing. "She's not her mother. She looks a hell of a lot like Vanessa, but that's where it ends."

Eli seemed to be considering his words.

"You heard from him?" Razor asked.

Slowly, Eli shook his head.

"Just another thought for you," Razor told him. "Selling her off might not have been his only play. You thought about that?"

"What are you saying?" Eli glared at him.

"You sure he's not going to move against *you*?" Razor watched some of that anger fade from his face. "Maybe him trying to sell Jade served a double purpose."

If it wouldn't have hurt like hell, Razor would have laughed at the combination of indignation and realization on the other man's face. "Baby Face still has some demons," Eli tried, "but I don't think he has it in him to come after *me*."

Razor shook his head. "Why? Because you're his father and he loves you so much?"

"Fuck you," Eli muttered.

The reaction told Razor that Eli knew there was a possibility he could be right. "We need to find him and those with him before this all goes to hell, Eli," Razor told him.

After a long moment, Eli looked up and met his

gaze. "Yeah. We do."

* * *

Jade

"Here we are," Hero told her as he let them in to the Hounds of Hell clubhouse. As he led her out of a larger room with a bar and a pool table set up, she noticed a lot of old photographs in framed collages on the wall. She made a mental note to have a look at those later.

When they went down a corridor, Hero stopped to unlock the door to what looked like an office. Once inside, she saw it was like a one-room apartment. There was a bed on one side of the room with a huge flat screen on the wall across from it. There were small bits of clutter here and there but for the most part, it was clean. There was a mini-fridge, a microwave, and a good-sized chest of drawers.

"I grabbed one of the rooms with a bathroom," Hero told her with a wink. "There's no shower, but I'll show you where those are."

Jade nodded. "What was this place?"

"Would you believe it used to be the Mercy police station?" Hero laughed at her expression. "Yeah, I get that. There are even jail cells. I'll show you those later."

"Is anyone else here?"

"Not right now," he told her, taking her things and setting them off to the side. "But they'll be here soon. You'll meet them."

"Am I the only woman… staying here?"

Hero put his arms around her, pulled her against him. He pressed kisses into her hair. "You are," he told her. "Just until it's safe for you to go back to your house."

He held her there for a moment and when she opened her eyes, she noticed more pictures. Some in framed groups, some tacked to the wall. Easing out of his arms, she walked over to them, smiling to see Hero when he was younger. "You played football?" she asked, pointing to a team picture with all of them in their jerseys.

There was the slightest change in his demeanor as he joined her, blowing out a sigh. "In high school. I played defensive line."

"Where did you get the name Hero?" She had to ask.

Instead of lightening the mood, it only made him seem to draw more in on himself. "Not from football," he said after a moment.

"Sorry." Jade decided to drop it.

"No, it's okay," he told her, pressing up behind her and wrapping his arms around her waist. "I had very different goals back then."

Jade's eyes scanned the pictures around the one of the football team. A group of them in summer clothes at the lake, another with more or less the same people at a party.

Hero had been so young then, his face softer than it was now.

She noticed his arm around another girl in a photo further down. She had flaming red curls framing a pale face littered with freckles. She was pretty, grinning at the camera with her arms around Hero's waist.

"That was my girlfriend the last two years of high school," he said. He'd followed the line of her gaze. "Maisie. The most popular girl in school. Her family had money. They lived around the lake back then. She and her friends had parties there almost every weekend."

The homes by the lake there in Mercy were beautiful and opulent. Once in a while they'd camped out at the lake once her grandma started seeing Emery. They'd ride bikes through those ritzy neighborhoods. Jade had always wondered what those homes looked like on the inside. What it was like to live there.

"She never gave me the time of day until I made it onto the football team," he went on. "Then she showed some interest. Had me thinking I could go to a big college like she was. That I could be somebody, you know?"

Hero's arms tightened around her. "A week before graduation, a bunch of us went to the lake. Swimming. There's a big cliff up there you could jump from."

Jade nodded. "I know it."

"You do?"

"I grew up here," she reminded him.

"Anyway, she slid on the rocks up there and didn't jump so much as she fell. Once she hit the water, she didn't come back up."

Her heart sped up as she listened.

"I dove in," Hero went on. "Got her up and out of the lake. Got her breathing again. Scared the shit out of me."

Jade crossed her arms over his. "But you saved her."

"Yeah."

"With witnesses," she pointed out.

Hero chuckled at that. "I did. I felt like I was about ten feet tall that day. The nickname stuck."

That wasn't the end though. She could feel it. It was a couple of beats before he continued. "We graduated and we went out most of that summer,"

Hero told her. "Until it was time for college in the fall. Then she went to college like she and her parents wanted, off to Boston."

"And you?"

"I stayed here," he told her. "My folks are good people, but they don't have anything. My younger brother ended up working his way up from community college but now he's got a shit ton of student loans he's never going to pay off."

Jade's heart clenched at the thought that his first love had left him. "Did she come back at all?" She was struggling to understand.

"She called once," Hero muttered. "So that's the story. It's not all that great, huh?"

Turning in his arms, Jade smiled up at him. "But you *are* a hero."

"I'm not the only one who could have dove in to save her."

"But you're the only one who could've saved me," she told him. "And you *did* save me. I'll never forget it."

Hero tightened his hold on her. "I kind of had to save you. You're Razor's daughter."

"That was the only reason?"

His lips pressed to hers, hot and demanding. She let him deepen the kiss and it took her breath away, left her hanging onto him, her fingers clutched in his hair. "I think you know better than that," he whispered.

Her world upended when he spun them around, pushing her on his bed. When he climbed on the bed after her, moving over her, his weight felt so good. His kisses were a fiery campaign over her mouth and neck. His hands sought out all the places that made her tremble and she was drugged by his kisses as he worked at stripping her bare.

Hero let her pull his cut and shirt off before he got his hands and mouth on her breasts. Jade's fingers twisted in his hair as she struggled to breathe, loving how he was careful with how he touched and loved her. His heated cock, encased in denim, pressed against her most intimate flesh and had her vining herself around him. She ached for him.

Hero was warm, his touch demanding. When he eased back to open his jeans and take them down, Jade surged up to get her hands and mouth on him. The cry she drew from him was satisfying as she explored the swollen head of him with her lips and tongue. With one hand she stroked his shaft while her other hand played with his balls, trying to learn what he liked.

All the while she teased him until she began to work him into her mouth. Hero's hands slid into her hair, clutching there but not trying to take control from her. His body tensed as she worked him, his moans a symphony that she could definitely get used to.

"You're so fucking good at that, Jade," he said quietly, his grip tightening in her hair until there was the slightest sting of pain.

It drove her on, made her want to bring him off that way. She took him as far back as she could, her hands moving while she did. She loved the way he fought her, the way he seemed barely able to resist fucking her face.

When she doubled down, wanting him to come, he gripped her head carefully, pulled her off him. "Not right now," he told her, leaning down to kiss her breathless.

Working his jeans off with impressive speed, Hero had her spread out beneath him on the bed the next beat. Her hands clutched at the bedding, his back, anything she could reach, as he began pushing into her. The burn as her body stretched around him was so good. When he pushed all the way in, it felt even better. She was so ready for him. So wet. Hero moved easily within her. Her thighs locked around his slim hips as his thrusts gained slowly in speed and strength. Her nails raked over the slick skin of his back as she moved with him, craving more of him deep inside her.

Their hearts beat in unison as they moved. When he slid a hand between them to delicately torment the pearl above where their bodies were joined, it intensified the rising swell of pleasure in her. "Hero," she managed, hanging onto him for dear life.

"Yeah?" Hero's breath came as fast as hers, heated pants over her face.

She couldn't answer. She was helpless beneath him, craving the release she so desperately needed. Her body clenched around him, her arms and legs tightened.

"That's it, baby," Hero whispered in her ear. "Give it to me."

And she did. Currents of pleasures bloomed in her pussy, flowing through her veins fiery and fast. Jade screamed and cried out as the room spun around her, as Hero's movements quickened. When he reached his own orgasm, his cries were guttural and echoing through the room.

They ended up in a sweaty pile on his bed, the rush of her breath as loud as his. His heart thundered beneath her ear when she rested her head on his chest. His arms were strong around her, holding her there. "Whatever happens, trust me," Hero told her. He sounded so tired. "I won't let anything happen to you. Our club, your father, we're all going to take care of you. Okay?"

Jade wanted so much to believe that even as she fought the fears lingering at the edges of her mind. "I trust you, Hero," she whispered. It was the only thing that felt right.

Chapter Seven

Jade

The sudden sharp rapping on the door startled Jade awake. She sat up, her heart racing in her chest.

"Hero?" a deep voice called from the beyond the door.

Hero's blue eyes slit open. "Snow?"

"Yeah. Trouble's coming."

"Shit," Hero muttered, jumping out of bed to fish his clothes from the floor.

Jade followed suit, dressing quickly. She watched Hero, his movements fast and determined. In seconds they were dressed, and Hero took her hand, pulling her out of his room. "Where are we going?" she asked, scared.

When they reached the main room of the building, it was filled with men wearing cuts like Hero and her father. She recognized the twins, tall and handsome with longer brown hair and blue-gray eyes.

"There they are," a taller man said. She recognized him as the biker who brought her father to the funeral.

"This is Snow." Hero gestured to him. "He's our VP."

Jade nodded as his gray eyes moved over her, smiling.

"You've met Axel and Ryder." Hero pointed to the twins.

"This is Razor's kid?"

Jade's gaze found the speaker, a tall muscular man with dark hair and darker eyes. Swarthy and powerful, he was almost as big as Hero, and his gaze was assessing and sharp. "She is," Hero told him. "This is Jade. Jade, this is Beast."

"Hero." Snow got their attention. "Emery sent us a tip."

Emery? *That wasn't good.* Her heart lurched in her chest.

"Said he got word that Baby Face is on the move. He's looking for *her*."

Hero's hand tightened around hers, lending her his strength.

"Now apparently he's told some of the other Cottonmouths some bullshit story," Snow went on. "They're coming with him. No sign of Big Dog but Jimmy Jazz is with him."

"Fuck," Hero muttered.

It was then she noticed all the guns and rifles covering the pool table. Boxes of ammo, a couple of knives.

"Wait, who's at the hospital with Razor?" Hero asked.

"Fuck that," a familiar voice came from behind them.

It was her father. Jade shook her head, pulling free of Hero's grip and heading for him. "You shouldn't be out of the hospital," she told him, her heart dropping to see the father she'd only just met looking so washed out and tired.

Lifting a hand to the side of her face, he smiled. "Probably not, but there was no way I was going to stay there with my girl in danger." Looking around her, Razor addressed the room. "I'm going to take Jade back to my office," he said, grabbing a rifle and a box of ammunition from the pool table behind her. "Hero, you and Snow set up in here. Cover the windows, monitor the cameras. Kick some ass."

As everyone started moving, Hero walked up to them. His gaze was on her. "You're going to be okay," he told her, smiling.

Razor's gazed moved from her to Hero and back again. He shook his head. "I fucking knew it," he said.

Jade's face warmed at the observation. Hero did manage to look chagrined.

"At least you didn't pick Snow," Razor told her.

Snow walked past them, flipping off his president.

"Move," Razor told them, leading Jade from the room.

* * *

Hero

The fear Hero read in Jade's expression had him determined to end the situation with Baby Face and the Cottonmouths. The look his president cut him as he led her away from him let him know they'd be having a talk once this was all done.

Yeah, he hadn't expected to start something with Razor's daughter and there'd be no questions asked. Still, if Razor had been all that opposed to the idea, he'd know. Their prez was anything but subtle. Right now, their job was to protect her and Razor. No matter what.

While Ryder watched the cameras, the rest of them got the windows covered and picked out positions. Hero took a position where he had a clear view of their main room and the hallway leading to Razor's office. Questions raced through his mind at lightning speed. What the hell had Baby Face told the rest of the Cottonmouths that had them all heading over here? He didn't know Emery Phillips all that well, but the man had sent them a message for a reason. If Emery had reason to think Jade might be in danger and that was good enough for Hero. He shook his head.

They were really going to do this at the Hound clubhouse?

The roar of engines got his attention, had him checking the window. A cluster of headlights was heading up the road. There were at least a dozen of them. *Fuck*. Did Eli know about this? Was he *with* them?

"They're here," Snow called.

Doing a quick head count, they had ten if you counted Razor. They were slightly outnumbered, but such odds never scared him. They'd handle it. Watching them park and scramble off their bikes, Hero waited. He felt ready for anything until a bottle crashed the window behind him, flames spreading from the rag in it to the floor.

"Shit!" he yelled, running to the bar, and grabbing the fire extinguisher from behind it. Two more flaming bottles crashed through other windows as he worked. He was grateful there were no windows in Razor's office.

While he watched, Jimmy Jazz launched himself through one of those windows, the floor in flames below him. Hero ran in his direction and let loose with the extinguisher to put out the flames, to spray it in Jazz's fucking face. Putting up his arms to deflect the blinding mist, Jazz dropped his handgun, yelling a string of obscenities as shots started ringing out.

While Jazz was swiping at his face with his hands, Hero bashed his head with the extinguisher. The other man yelled as he went down, straining to gaze up at him.

"How's the shoulder?" Hero asked before knocking him out with the next blow.

Beast and one of the prospects grabbed the other two fire extinguishers as the Cottonmouths forced their way in through the broken windows. From there it was chaos, bullets and fists flying.

Hero didn't even know the name of the asshole who'd gotten an arm around his neck, trying to choke him out. He moved fast, flipping him over a shoulder before he started landing blows. The younger man wasn't as brave face-to-face and caved pretty quickly.

His gaze swept the room when the sound of gunfire died down. The twins were beating the shit out of people, Snow kicked one of the older Cottonmouths in the face, and he saw several Cottonmouth prospects. Just maybe it was a good sign that he didn't see a lot of familiar faces from the MC. Maybe that meant Baby Face just duped a bunch of the new ones.

Baby Face. Finally, he spotted the bastard responsible for all of this. His knives were out, and he was easily cutting up one of the Hound prospects. Hero liked the kid. But it gave him just the opportunity he wanted. He reached them just as Baby Face's blade sliced open the kid's upper arm. The other man's pretty face lit up to see the line of blood, the kid's horrified look.

Hero stepped in front of him, facing down Baby Face.

"There you are." Baby Face's malevolent smile didn't reach his eyes.

"Here I am," Hero told him, sizing up the man who tried to sell Razor's daughter. *His* Jade.

Baby Face came at him with the knives, his movements swift and calculated. Hero was careful, keeping an eye on those knives and trying to decide how he could take the little fucker down. The other man moved too fast for him to grab him or try to disarm him. He was also a head shorter than Hero, his swipes aimed at his torso.

They danced around each other while the fighting raged on all around them. Hero dodged some of his swipes, tried to grab for him.

Baby Face's unblinking stare was a little unnerving. The longer their dance continued, the more gleeful he looked. He was too focused and too capable with his blades.

"How's Big Dog?" Hero asked, grinning. "He found a good plastic surgeon yet?"

The little bastard snarled at him. "You destroyed his jaw. And you're going to pay for that."

Hero dodged another swipe, got lucky and landed a punch at his jaw. It was satisfying to watch Baby Face stumble back, to have that moment of doubt. "I'm not the one who put him there, am I?" Hero asked, coming damn close to grabbing his left arm when he shoved it at his midsection. "You are."

"Don't be so dramatic, Hero," Baby Face told him with a smile. "You fucked up his face but he's going to live. I promised him I'd get him some payback."

"He'll be disappointed." Hero kicked one of his legs out from under him, sending Baby Face tumbling to the floor. While he was off balance, Hero stomped on his right wrist. When the other man cried out in pain, Hero kicked that blade away. Leaning in, he landed solid punches to the Cottonmouth's chin, his nose.

When the shine off his other blade caught his eye, Hero moved just in time to avoid the point sinking into his eye. With an enraged scream, Baby Face managed to climb to his feet, coming after him. "You should have minded your own fucking business!" Baby Face yelled. "Had nothing to do with you, Hero!"

That blade sliced the meat of his forearm. The

sting only motivated him. "She's Razor's daughter," Hero told him, making Baby Face dodge his left hook. "That makes it very much my fucking business."

Baby Face paused then, considering his words. "What makes you an authority on who fathered that little bitch?"

"What's the matter? Worried about the consequences if you're fucking wrong?" Hero swung at him again with his left but caught him with his right. When Baby Face stumbled back into the pool table, Hero rushed him. He twisted his wrist until he felt something snap, until he released the other silver blade. Then Hero started beating the shit out of him.

It was Baby Face's lucky fucking day. A familiar voice yelled, "Enough!"

Everything came to a stop as they all looked to the newcomer in the now open doorway. It was Eli.

The menace faded from his son's battered face as Eli headed for them. "What fucking lie did you tell them?" Eli demanded. Before his son could manage to pull himself up on the pool table, his father shoved Hero out of the way and grabbed Baby Face by the front of his shirt. "What the fuck did you tell your brothers to make them come here and pull this shit for you?" When his son just stared at him, he yelled, "Answer!"

"They shot Jimmy," Baby Face tried. "They fucked up Big Dog's face big time."

"And why did they do that?" the other club's president asked.

With hope creeping into his expression, Baby Face cut his gaze to Hero and back to his father. "They interfered with our business," Baby Face said with no small measure of indignation.

"The business of selling your sister?"

Oh, the fear returned to the young man's face with a vengeance. "What?"

"Your sister," Eli said loudly. "Did you sell her to Big Billy?"

With his mouth hanging open, his lip bloody, Baby Face shook his head.

"You know what makes this fucking worse?" Eli asked. "That girl ain't your damn sister. She's not mine. She's Razor's."

Hero crossed his arms across his chest. *She's mine.*

Knowing everyone was listening, Baby Face started curling in on himself.

"You took your knife to Razor when he was just trying to protect his daughter," Eli went on. "You tried to turn her out at Big Billy's and then you lied about it all. I miss anything?"

Baby Face knew he had nowhere to go. Knew he was screwed. "Don't I get to tell my side?" It was the last card he had to play.

"About the fucking gambling debts?" Eli's fury colored his weathered face red. "About the goons looking for your sorry ass for weeks?"

Baby Face dropped his gaze. He knew it was over now.

"You make me fucking sick," Eli muttered. "You're a stain on our MC."

No one expected him to pull the gun, point it at his son's face.

"You can't --"

Eli pulled the trigger, putting the bullet in his son's head. He didn't show a sliver of remorse as he watched the life leave his son on the pool table.

"Eli," Razor reached them, his expression grave.

"You were right," Eli told him.

Hero could tell the admission wasn't easy with him.

"Does this conclude our business?" Eli asked.

It was the closest thing they'd get to an apology from the other president.

"Yeah," Razor told him.

Hero glanced around the room. Jimmy Jazz was out cold but alive. He saw a couple other Cottonmouths down but there was movement. There were injuries. And they had a hell of a lot of repair work to do here at the club house. At least the place hadn't gone up in flames. But that was the end of it.

Eli turned and headed back the way he'd come. There were other Cottonmouths, ones Hero recognized who'd arrived with Eli. Two of them came for Baby Face's body, more rounding up the others.

"Where's Jade?" Hero asked her father.

Razor tipped his head in the direction of the office. Hero headed in that direction but Razor's hand on his shoulder stopped him.

Hero paused at the look in his president's eyes.

"What are your intentions with my daughter?" Razor asked seriously. "I spent years unable to even talk to her. I'm not allowing any stupid shit to interfere now that I have a chance to get to know her."

So many things came to mind to say, and Hero hesitated. Snow walked up, his grin sly. "Looks like he's got it bad." Snow laughed. "Don't you, Hero?"

Well, that wasn't a lie.

"That true?" Razor asked him.

"It's early," Hero admitted. "But I'm not playing."

Razor sized him up in a way he hadn't since he was a prospect. After a moment, he nodded. "It's not going to go well if you fuck up," Razor warned him.

"Then I'm going to try hard not to." Hero meant it.

With that meaningful conversation done, Hero headed for Razor's office. Jade's eyes were wide on him when he pulled open the door. "It's over," he told her.

His Jade jumped up from the chair, flew into his arms. Hero liked how she felt in his embrace.

"Is everyone okay?"

"Our people are, yeah," he told her.

That had her easing back to glance up at him. "What about…"

"He's dead." Hero wanted her to know. "His father took him out. You're safe now."

When she stretched up to kiss him, Hero lost himself in her scent and taste. Now that they'd made sure she was safe, he needed to figure out how he was going to keep her.

Epilogue

Jade

When Jade woke up the next morning, she was alone. Her first reaction was fear but then she remembered. Baby Face was dead. The business between his club and her father's was over. She was safe.

Where was Hero?

Sitting up, she stretched. Wearing nothing but one of his T-shirts, she threw her legs over the side. Oh, she was sore in odd places. Some of it was from the chaos of the last few days. Some of it was Hero. That had her grinning.

Jade showered and dressed, heading down to figure out breakfast. She also needed to consider where she was going to go from here. As she picked out a sympathy casserole, she considered freezing some of the others. It was almost lunchtime.

She started thinking about her apartment in Providence. Surely now that she wasn't in danger she could go back to Providence and decide what to do. She'd either clear out her apartment, say her goodbyes, and settle in here in her childhood home or she'd stay there, try to find a job, and start her life. Sure, the cost of living would be higher in Providence but there were more opportunities for work there.

Her heart squeezed in her chest as she thought about returning to Providence. It wasn't what her heart wanted.

She'd almost finished her brunch when someone knocked on the door. Jade was happy to see Emery there on her doorstep, and she hugged him. "Thank you for getting word to the guys," she told him, walking him into the living room.

Emery's eyes were shiny. "I was worried sick. What happened?"

Knowing Emery shared her grandmother's distaste for all things biker-related, Jade edited her story. The Hounds, she explained, were ready when the Cottonmouths arrived. Then Eli showed up to make peace and it was all settled.

Jade knew she must have done a bad job on her composed story because the older man didn't look convinced. "Where's Baby Face?" Emery asked.

No way she was explaining that. "He won't be a problem anymore," she told him. "It's all done."

Nodding, he dropped his gaze. She knew what was coming, knew what he was going to say. "Jade, go back to Providence," he told her meaningfully. "I'll miss you terribly, just like I'll miss Mina. But you can come to visit me. Just go back there. You'll be safer there."

Reaching for his hand, Jade smiled. "I appreciate you looking out for me," she told him. "Since I've been here, I have a better idea of why my grandmother wanted me away from the MCs."

"Then you know why she was right," Emery replied. "It's what's best for you."

"What's best for me is getting to know my father," she told him carefully. "He's not a bad guy, Emery. You and he are all the family I have left now."

Emery looked chagrined but let her finish.

"I'm going to go to Providence and clean out my apartment. Tie up loose ends. Then I'm going to move here. At least for now."

He didn't look happy, but what could he do really? She was an adult, and it was her life. "Just think about it," he said finally. "You said you had a couple of weeks, right? Just think it over."

Jade nodded. She warmed up some casserole for him, and they enjoyed a meal together, talked about Mina. When it was time for him to go, she hugged him goodbye. After cleaning up the kitchen, she went for her laptop, wanting to catch up on everything. Since the Cottonmouths took her phone, she'd been out of touch with everyone left in her life.

Her heart lurched when the door just opened this time, but she wasn't all that surprised to see Hero walking into the kitchen, grinning at her. Leaning down he brushed a kiss on her cheek before sitting a small box on the table by her laptop.

Jade grinned up at him. "What's this?"

"Open it."

When she pulled the top off the box, she saw Hero brought her a new phone. It was much nicer than anything she'd ever chosen for herself. "Thank you," she told him.

"Just need to set up service," he told her.

Jade needed to call her provider anyway since her phone had been stolen.

Joining her at the table, Hero's gaze was assessing. "How are you feeling?"

"I'm just fine." She was. "Where have you been?"

"Housekeeping," he told her. "Had to get Razor set up at home since he won't keep his ass at the hospital."

That had her laughing with him.

"And we have a lot of cleaning up to do at the clubhouse. We have busted windows, bullet holes, and the floor's fucked up," he explained. "So when I'm not at work, I'm going to be helping there until we get it all fixed."

That reminded her. "You have a job?"

Hero nodded. "Yeah, I do. I work at a body shop

in town."

"So you're an artist?"

He shook his head. "I wouldn't go that far, but I can make a car look pretty damn good."

She didn't doubt that.

Hero sat watching her and she waited. "What are *your* plans, Jade?" he asked.

"I just had this conversation with Emery a little while ago."

Hero looked less confident now, shook his head.

"I still need to go back to Providence," she told him. "I still have time to clear everything out and wrap everything up. But then, I'm going to move in here. Give Mercy a try."

The smile she loved was forming on his face. "Yeah?"

Jade couldn't help but answer that smile. She nodded. "I just started talking to my father," she went on, reaching for his hand. "Then there's this guy…"

"A guy, huh?" Hero took her hand, using it to pull her out of her chair and into his lap. She'd barely gotten her arms around his neck when his mouth claimed hers, his kiss careful at first. The hard ridge of him beneath her got her attention, especially when his hips nudged up against her.

When those heated lips and the scruff of his beard blazed a trail across to her jaw and down to her neck, she gasped as currents of pleasure raced through her. His whisper in her ear had her shivering in his arms. "You gonna stay in Mercy with me?"

His rough hands were already hauling the skirt of her summer dress up, manhandling her until she was straddling him. It seemed effortless for him to push the chair away from the table to give them more room. When his hands made it under her skirt, and he was kissing her breathless all the while, they twisted in the soft cotton of her panties which gave with a quiet ripping sound.

No sooner had he dropped them to the floor when his hand was working to open his jeans, to push them down his hips just enough. The scent of her own arousal rose on the heat of their bodies, had her clenching for him. When he had himself in hand, she moved with him, easing herself down on his cock, craving the way it filled her.

Hero let her take him at her own pace. The harsh rasp of their breathing was the only sound and her heart was racing in her chest as he slid home inside her. She ground her lower body down on him. He felt so good...

His kisses continued, peppering over her face and heating up her lips. Feverishly they worked together, Hero's hands on her hips moving her up and down his cock. Her fingers clutched at his hair, the back of his leather cut.

"Stay with me," he whispered against her lips, his thrusts gaining in speed and strength. "Stay with me, Jade."

Jade had never been with someone who could make her feel like he did. As her inner muscles tightened around him and pleasure swelled within her, she rode the wave. She loved the way his lips caressed her neck and ears, the careful way he handled her. The sharp thrusts of his hips were an indecent counterpoint to the gentle rain of his kisses. He pushed her over the edge first, had her crying out as her thighs locked around him and orgasm shook her. Hero muttered her name as he pulled her down on him, again and again, fighting to reach his own end. She was limp against him when he tightened around her, pumping up into her in a frenzy as he unloaded.

When she came back around, she was draped over him, trying to breathe. They were still joined, and he didn't seem to be in a hurry to change that. His fingers traced circuits over her back as they held each other. "Now can I go with you to Providence?" he asked, pressing a kiss into her hair. "Not because you need me to…"

"Because I want you to?" Easing back to see his face, Jade smiled. "Yes, I think I'd like that."

The kiss they shared was gentle, a promise sealed by lips and hope.

Something occurred to her. "Will my father be okay while we're gone?"

Hero nodded, brushing a kiss on her forehead. "It would take a lot to stop Razor. He's one tough son of a bitch."

"There's so much I don't know about your world," she admitted.

"I'll tell you anything," Hero told her. "As long as I get to keep you."

Jade wasn't about to tell him yet. But she very much wanted him to keep her.

Snow (Hounds of Hell MC 2)
A Hounds of Hell MC Romance
Jamie Targaet

Emily -- Most wonderful time of the year? Yeah, right. Business isn't booming at my bakery this Christmas and I'm behind on my business loan. And if that weren't enough, my SUV's transmission is dying, my ex is in town for the holidays, and our regular Santa broke his leg and can't make it for the annual children's Christmas party. Somehow, we've ended up with a biker playing Santa Claus this year and I think he's the wrong man for the job. Santa shouldn't have all those muscles and tattoos. I shouldn't be daydreaming about sitting in Santa's lap.

Snow -- I'm not a man with a sweet tooth -- at least I wasn't until now. If I'd known about the gorgeous little baker, I'd have snatched her up years ago. The little lady has a lot of problems this holiday season. For her, I'll play Santa Claus for the kids, and her ex will wish he got a lump of coal in his stocking when I'm done with him. Emily will have a good Christmas. I guaran-damn-tee it.

Chapter One

Emily

"Wait. What?" Emily Frost couldn't have heard that right. The annual Christmas event they held in Mercy each year for the town's children was two weeks away. "What do you mean Andy isn't going to be able to play Santa Claus this year?"

While she listened to the elderly man's wife explain why he wouldn't be able to be Santa this year, Emily was fighting off hysteria. She understood that he'd taken a nasty fall and told his wife she was very sorry he'd broken his leg. Automatically, she asked if there was anything she could do. She *did* care. But she really wasn't listening for a response.

What was she going to do?

Emily carried on the rest of the conversation as best she could, taking a deep breath when she ended the call.

"Fuck!" Her yell echoed through the quiet bakery.

Could things get any worse? She was blinking back tears as she finished counting the register and got all the goodies that hadn't sold today boxed up. And there was a *lot* that hadn't sold today.

The planning committee for the Christmas event was meeting tomorrow. Each member of that committee had jobs to do to make the event happen each year. Liza Austin and her husband owned a greenhouse in town. Each year they provided a beautiful wreath for the door. A live potted Christmas tree for the event was displayed in her bakery shop's window throughout the holidays. Liza had a key to the shop to take care of the tree so it could be replanted later.

Myra Michaels handled the guest list, answering questions from parents and guardians about the event. She also handled donations that came in. Mina Dock had passed away this summer, but her granddaughter had moved back to town and was taking her place on the committee. Jade Dock and Emery Phillips oversaw setup, using folding chairs and tables Emery used at his bar, Sackett's, for special events. They got out the decorations they used each year. Most had been donated by Jade's grandmother Mina.

Emily had been a part of the committee since its first year, five years ago. Her job was supplying all the baked goods for the event and, with help, filling stockings with candy and treats for the kids to take home.

And she'd been the one who found their Santa Claus, Andy Wilder. Each year the elderly gentleman arrived as Santa and was just the best part of the entire event in her opinion. His warmth and sincerity made him a perfect choice. Plus, he could handle anything, from kids scared of Santa to those who were acting up and rowdy.

But he wasn't coming this year. That was just the latest calamity this week and it was just Thursday night.

Where were they going to get another Santa Claus with two weeks to go?

Locking the door on her way out, she carried the box of goodies out to her SUV and got in. Emily crossed her fingers that the damn thing would start because it hadn't been running right for the last several weeks. She knew her transmission was failing. What she didn't know, since things had been so slow at the shop, was where she was getting the money to fix it.

In five minutes, she reached Mercy's homeless

shelter, delivering what she didn't sell as she did every day the bakery was open. Heading for the back door, Emily rounded the corner and almost collided with someone.

"I'm sorry," she muttered glancing up into gray eyes.

There were two men, both tall and wearing leather vests with their biker gang name on them, carrying a bed frame into the shelter. The one closest to the door was blond and nice-looking. The one she almost ran into? He was just as tall and muscular, with a dark beard and mustache and almost entirely white locks of hair in disarray on his head. She did a double take because hair that color didn't usually go with a younger face. His eyes were pale gray and stunning.

The Hounds of Hell had long been a part of Mercy according to Liza, and she spoke of them fondly. Emily didn't know much about motorcycle gangs and none of them ever came to her bakery. She really wanted to keep it that way. They were a little scary for her.

That gray-eyed gaze moved over her until the blond lost patience. "Snow, we still moving this frame?"

Snow returned his attention to the task, and someone else walked over to her.

"Emily, how are you?" Jade Dock asked. "Making your deliveries?"

Emily smiled. "I am. How are you?"

"Donating some things," Jade said, watching the men carry the bed frame carefully through the shelter door. "At least I have some strong help to move them."

Jade walked with her into the shelter. As she always did, Emily placed the box of treats on the receptionist's desk just inside.

"Who's your friend?" a deep voice behind her asked.

"Oh, I'm sorry. Guys, this is Emily," Jade said, motioning to the two bikers who were apparently with her. To Emily, she said, "This is Hero and Snow."

Emily shook hands with both, noticing the one she called Snow wasn't too quick to release her hand. By the time he did, she noticed the blond had his arm around Jade's waist. So they were a couple?

"I'd better get going," Emily said. "It's nice meeting you."

"I'll see you at the meeting tomorrow?" Jade called as she walked back to the SUV.

When I get to tell the committee we need another Santa Claus, and we just have two weeks to find one? Yes, wouldn't miss it.

"I'll see you there," Emily said over her shoulder as she reached the door. And as she headed back to her SUV, she just hoped the damn thing would start and not embarrass her in front of the bikers.

* * *

Snow

August Crowe, Snow to his MC, watched the petite blonde rush back to her SUV, the long braid of her hair dancing behind her. She looked so perky in her soft sweater and form-hugging slacks. He'd never seen an ass like that on such an uppity girl.

"Who's that?" Snow asked Jade as he helped Hero get the old box spring out of the truck bed.

Jade watched her drive away in her SUV before turning back to Snow. "That's Emily Frost. She owns Whisk and Whimsy in town. It's a bakery."

Frost, huh? That had Snow grinning. They sounded like a matched pair.

"Say *that* five times really fast," Hero said from the other side of the furniture they were moving.

Figures. She looked like someone you'd find in a bakery, making treats. If he thought she'd give him the time of day, Snow would become a bakery patron real fucking fast. But from the look she cut him, he probably wouldn't have a lot of luck.

"What meeting is tomorrow?" Hero asked Jade, holding one end of the box spring and guiding Snow who carried the other.

"Planning committee for the annual kids' Christmas party," Jade explained. "It's only two weeks away."

Jade had mentioned it recently. Doing an event for the poor kids in Mercy sounded like a good plan to him. If Miss Uppity was in on it, she had a good heart.

"If you need help with that, let me know," Snow said. It earned him a look from both Jade and Hero, but he meant it. There had been a few times when he'd been a kid that he and his family wouldn't have had food if not for the kindness of others. He liked the idea of paying it forward.

"Thank you, Snow," Jade told him. "I'll keep that in mind."

Hero shook his head as they reached the shelter door.

"What?" Snow asked. "Something wrong with wanting to help kids? Razor did say we should do some community outreach."

"Not that," Hero said. "The blonde. I'd forget that if I were you."

"Why?" Jade asked. "Emily's nice."

"Maybe so," Hero said. "But I'd be willing to bet someone in an MC isn't exactly her type."

"I might have said the same thing once," Jade

didn't look convinced. "You can't assume things like that."

She had a point.

"So the party is for *any* kid in Mercy?" Snow asked as they maneuvered the box spring through the shelter door.

Jade followed them. "Technically. We have to leave it open for anyone to avoid singling people out, you know? The ones who really need help."

"Good approach," Snow said.

"I'm told each year we have a tree and decorations. There's an older man who comes to play Santa Claus. There are treats for everyone and everyone gets a gift from Santa. We identify the kids who really need help and they get different gifts than the ones we give the other kids that show up."

"Makes sense," Snow said. "What do the poor kids get?"

"The smaller ones get a toy, some candy, and a gift card this year," Jade explained. "The older kids get candy and a bigger gift card. Santa tells them they can't open their presents until Christmas Eve. Liza said *most* of the time that works."

It was thoughtful.

They set the box spring down, heading back out for the mattress.

"Offer stands," Snow said to Jade. "Let me know if I can help. Even if it's just setup."

"Okay, thank you, Snow," Jade said.

* * *

Emily

"What do you mean we have no Santa?" Liza Austin asked from the other side of the table in the prep room of Emily's bakery. The owner of the town's plant nursery wore her gray curls pulled back in a ponytail, confusion creeping into her expression. "Is Andy okay?"

"He fell," Emily explained. "His wife called yesterday to let us know that he'd recover but his leg was broken. In two places. I guess he's going to need surgery and yeah… Right now, we have no Santa."

Myra Michaels shook her head in her seat next to Emily. The fluorescent lights above winked off the white strands running all through the fading red of her hair. She stared at Emily over the rims of her glasses. "What about Emery?"

That had everyone looking to the only man on the committee, sitting next to Jade. Emery was a smaller man with white hair and bright blue eyes. The man would blow away in a strong breeze. He had to be in his late seventies, and he was rail thin.

"I don't think that would work," Jade said. "We have the costume. We just need someone bigger to fit it."

"True," Liza said. "Andy's a pretty big guy."

Jade nodded. "He is. We need to find someone taller. We can pad him up."

Emily put it on her list under "immediate needs." Reviewing the rest of the list, they appeared to be in good shape. "Okay, do we have all the donations in?"

Myra nodded. "We do. So, if we agree, I can organize that shopping trip."

Every year, Liza and Myra were trusted with the money they budgeted for the gifts. Every year, Emily was so grateful they did.

"Oh, I'll need help the night before to get all the treats wrapped and ready," Emily reminded them. "If any of you could help, I'd appreciate it."

Jade put her hand up. "I'll help."

"Thank you," she said. "Anyone else?"

Jade scanned the table just like she did, then said, "I can bring Hero too."

Her biker boyfriend. Well, he wasn't hard to look at and she did need help.

"Thank you," Emily told her. "I could use both of you."

When no one said anything else, Emily said, "Okay, so we need a Santa as soon as we can get one. I'll call the photographer and make sure he can be here this year. Is there anything else?"

After a moment, Jade put her hand up. "I might know someone who would work as Santa."

"That would be great," Emily said. "Who?"

Jade smiled. "A member of Hounds. Snow. He offered yesterday to help with the event if we needed him and he would probably fit the costume."

Liza nodded. "That he would. He's a good guy."

Emily held up a hand. "Jade, I really appreciate the offer but -- I don't know."

Hoping everyone would think about it a moment, Emily waited. She'd met "Snow," whatever his real name was, yesterday. She had someone different in mind to play Santa Claus. Someone older.

Someone who wasn't a member of a biker gang.

But all eyes were then on *her*. Emily cleared her throat. "We'll take a few suggestions and maybe meet in a week to agree on one," she offered.

"If Snow's willing to do it," Liza said, "we won't need other suggestions. Jade's right. Snow would do a good job. He's good with kids."

Myra nodded her agreement. Only Emery looked concerned.

"Snow's not a bad fella," Emery said. "I've

known him for years. It's just I don't think some of the townsfolks here will take kindly to having a biker as Santa Claus for their kids."

Jade was staring him down. "Most of the townsfolk you're talking about wouldn't even recognize him, Emery. He'd be fine."

Liza nodded. "That's right. Oh, and let him know he'll have to shave for this. We'll have a big white beard glue on and spirit gum in his whiskers would hurt like hell."

"Wait," Emily tried to break in. "We haven't even voted on this and --"

"Okay," Jade said. "All in favor of Snow being this year's Santa Claus, raise your hand."

Jade, Myra, and Liza all raised their hands while she and Emery just looked at each other.

"I'll talk to Snow as soon as the meeting is over," Jade said, smiling.

Emily shook her head, unhappy with how that had gone. "I don't even know his actual name." She realized she sounded dangerously close to whining.

"You know, I don't either," Jade said. "I'll find out. Liza, can I bring him here tomorrow evening so you can fit him?"

"Yep," Liza said. "Text me. The sooner I can make adjustments, the better."

With everything for the event discussed, they adjourned the meeting. Emily watched Jade and Liza talk excitedly about this year's Santa Claus.

Just when she thought the week couldn't get worse, it did. A biker from the Hounds of Hell as Santa? As Emily gathered her notebook and pen, she shook her head.

Andy had been the perfect Santa ever since they'd started the yearly event. He'd recently retired from teaching at the local community college their first year. Andy was older, well-spoken. The man was a father and a grandfather.

The biker was mostly an unknown. Emily didn't know how well Jade knew the man, but she knew nothing about him. She'd never seen him in Mercy before that she was aware of. After all, the man *was* really handsome. She would remember seeing *him* before.

While she knew on some level that it wasn't fair, she just couldn't get around the fact that the man belonged to a gang. Yes, his hair was white, even though he was younger, and maybe he'd fit in the suit. But was he well-spoken enough? Was he really good with kids? How would he handle the situations that came up every year?

Emily didn't like it. Not at all.

As she headed back to the front of her bakery, she sighed. It wasn't a done deal, she told herself, trying to relax. They had to ask the man first. Emily really couldn't see a biker being willing to play Santa. Even if he was, shaving off his facial hair could be a deal-breaker.

Taking a deep breath, she decided to get back to work and put it out of her mind until something was definite.

* * *

Snow

"You're really going to be Santa Claus for the event?" Jade asked for the third time, standing by the desk where he and Hero sat in the body shop's office.

"Definitely," Snow told her. "What all's involved?"

That stopped Jade. "I haven't been to one

because they started after I left for college. But from what I gather, you'll dress up as Santa and the little kids will come up, tell you what they want for Christmas, and get their picture taken."

"Do I need to buy a suit?" he asked.

"No, there's a Santa suit at the bakery," Jade said. "If you could, we need to fit you in the suit and figure out if we have to make alterations. Is there any way you can come to the bakery tomorrow evening?"

Bakery, huh?

Snow grinned. "Sure. I'll make it work."

"There's one more thing," Jade told him, looking very much like she was dreading what she was going to say next. "Liza said you'll need to be clean-shaven because they're going to glue on a white beard that goes with the suit."

"Glue?"

Hero snorted as he continued going over the shop schedule.

"Yeah," Jade was less confident. "She said they use spirit gum and if they put that on your facial hair, it'll hurt when you go to pull it off."

"No shit," Snow said with a laugh. "Fine. For the kids."

For the uppity little baker.

"Thank you." Jade was clearly relieved. "Can you meet me at the bakery tomorrow around six? Liza will be there too."

"Will anyone else be there?" He had to ask.

"Emily?" Jade's expression was knowing. "Yes. The shop stays open until six."

Snow nodded. "I'll definitely be there."

And he would. He'd even get there a little early to see if he could chat with the cute little blonde owner.

Chapter Two

Emily

It had been a busy day at Whisk and Whimsy, and she needed *that*. It had been surprisingly slow since Thanksgiving. Normally, Christmas was a crazy busy time of year.

Maybe the cinnamon roll wreaths she'd added were a good idea. She'd almost sold all of them today, so she decided to get to the bakery early tomorrow morning to make another batch. She'd been so absorbed in searching for other holiday recipes she didn't immediately realize someone walked into the shop.

It was the whistling that got her attention. Emily jumped up from the chair and hustled to the front. She stopped behind the display case when she saw who had walked into her bakery.

Disappointment stung as she realized that Snow, the biker, was here for one reason: he was volunteering to be Santa Claus for this year's event. Not only that, he'd already shaved his face.

That stopped her cold. While Emily hadn't known a lot of bikers in her life -- okay *any* -- she still found him attractive in a ruffian-like way. His mostly white hair was an interesting contrast to a younger face, but he looked to be maybe in his thirties. There were a few fine lines around those gray eyes. The dark beard had been another interesting contrast but without it... The man had a dip in his chin, a jawline for days. His face without the beard went from attractive to really striking.

The rest of him wasn't bad either. He was tall, broad-shouldered and muscular --

"Emily?"

Oh, shit. Am I staring?

"Hi," Emily said, flustered, and trying to put on her business face. "What can I get for you?"

Then he smiled. The bastard smiled at her, and she wasn't prepared for that. Where did a biker get perfect teeth like that? *Damn.*

"I don't think I've ever been in here before," Snow said, his voice whiskey deep. "What's good?"

Emily huffed at that. "I think everything is good. But I might be biased."

"You think so?" He winked at her. "I'm thinking I'll have a cinnamon roll wreath and a glazed cranberry orange scone." Snow laughed. "I don't even know what a fucking scone is."

Opening the back of the case, she put on a pair of gloves to get his order.

"Scones are actually like a flaky leavened bread," she explained. "Those are good choices for someone who didn't know what a scone was."

Snow shrugged a shoulder. "Obvious choice. If something's really good, at the end of the day it's going to be sold out or low in stock."

Emily wrapped each one and put them in a bag for him, moving to the register.

Snow moved down to the register, grinning like something was funny. Before she could enter either item on the screen, she met that gray-eyed gaze. "What?"

"I'm the new Santa Claus this year," Snow said. "Doesn't that earn me anything?"

Emily knew she wouldn't like this arrangement. Blowing out an exhale, she said, "Sure."

Snow took the small bag from her, pulling out the scone and unwrapping it. Standing right there on the other side of the counter, he bit into the treat. Emily felt awkward watching him eat it, looking around for something she could be doing.

"Well, that's pretty damn good," Snow said, before taking another bite.

"Thank you," Emily said. The fact that he liked what she made had her heart clenching in her chest. "I guess you're here to see if the suit will work?"

He'd eaten the scone quickly, swiping at his mouth with the back of his hand. Nodding, he said, "Yeah, here to meet Jade and Liza to try it on."

Checking her watch, Emily saw it was 5:45. "They aren't going to be here until six."

"Well, you're open until six, so I'll just hang out," he said.

Of course he will.

Nodding, she intended to head back to her office and her search for recipes.

"Tell me about this event," he called, taking a seat at one of her small tables and looking ridiculously large in the scrolly white chair. "Jade knew some details. But she hasn't been to one. She just moved here."

"She just moved *back*," Emily said, returning to the counter. "Jade grew up here. Mina Dock's granddaughter."

Snow nodded, his gaze roaming over her. "That's right."

"Anyway," Emily said, "the Christmas parties are nice. We have a lot of folks show up. More each year. The pandemic hit everyone hard."

"You survived," Snow pointed out.

Emily nodded. "There were a couple of times I didn't think I could keep the store open but somehow, I made it."

"You have to lay anyone off? Or did you get one

of those loans from the government?" he asked.

"I don't have employees," she told him. "Just me."

His dark brows rose. "One woman show?"

"Yes," Emily replied. It had always been that way.

"Your sign says you're open six days a week," Snow said.

"That's right." Since it was close to closing time and he seemed to want to talk, she started boxing up what she had left for the shelter.

"One day off a week? Do you take vacation time?" he asked.

Why was he so interested in her? Worse, why was she so flustered?

"I take time off during the holidays," she said, wanting to divert the conversation away from her. "Like Christmas. The party for the kids is a great event and it's really important to the community."

Snow nodded.

"Santa Claus is the most important part of it," she went on. He needed to know. "At least for the smaller kids. Do you have experience with kids?"

"I have a couple of little nephews next door in Franklin County. I do well enough with them, I guess."

"Good, because whoever plays Santa needs to be patient, and well-mannered. And there are a lot of special situations too."

"Special situations, huh?" Sitting back in the chair, he exhaled. "Like what?"

"Some kids are scared of Santa," Emily said. "Some have special needs. Santa has to handle everyone with patience and kindness, no matter what."

"And you have some doubts about my ability to handle all that, right?" Snow asked.

Not wanting to know what color she was turning from being called out, she scrambled for how to answer him. But he beat her to the punch.

"If it will help you sleep better at night," he said, "I assure you that I will be patient and jolly and Santa-like. As much as I can, padded up with a beard glued to my face anyway."

"It won't keep me up at night." How dare the handsome bastard insinuate that?

"Does thinking about me normally keep you up at night?" he asked, grinning.

Shaking her head, she crossed her arms over her chest. "I don't even know you."

"You will."

"We're working on this important community event," she told him. "That's all."

The smug grin stayed in place. "How long have you lived in Mercy?"

Emily didn't like all the questions. "Just about seven years," she said.

Snow nodded. "From the Midwest, judging by that accent."

"Michigan," she said.

"Mercy is my hometown," he went on. "I can't recall us ever having a bakery before."

"To my knowledge, there wasn't one," Emily replied. "It was one of things I was looking for. A town that didn't have a bakery."

"And you pulled it off by yourself," Snow said.

"If there had been a bakery before, would you have visited?" Emily asked.

Snow's smile widened. "If the bakery's owner looked like you? Absolutely."

The door opening had both of them looking up to see Liza and Jade rushing in, smiles in place.

"Snow, you're here early," Jade said. "Ready for your fitting?"

He nodded and followed the two women to the back of her shop.

"The costume is hung up on the storage room door," Emily called as the three of them headed in that direction.

* * *

Snow

As soon as Jade closed the door to the bakery's extra room, her attention was on Snow. "I knew it."

Snow kept smiling. "Knew what?"

"You were in here flirting with Emily," Jade said.

He wasn't going to deny it.

"Not that it will do me any good," Snow said. He watched Jade pull the Santa suit off the back of the door while Liza reached into her cross-body bag, pulling out a measuring tape and a small, cheap sewing kit.

"Why not?" Liza asked.

"I don't think I'm Betty Crocker's type," Snow said.

"Who?" Jade asked.

Liza shook her head. "You're a 'bad boy'." She put air quotes on the last two words. "Every woman is interested in the bad boy."

Snow shook his head. "I'm an air quotes bad boy? Really? That's all I get?"

"It is," Liza said as Jade took Santa's coat off the hanger. "I've known you since you were a kid, August. You can play the part, but deep down, you're good people."

Liza Austin and his mother had been close friends for years. Yeah, the woman who owned the town's garden center and greenhouse knew most everything about him. Including the bad stuff. Snow was just very grateful she wasn't a gossip.

"Don't tell *her* that," Snow told her with a wink.

"I agree," Jade said. "Things will be better with Emily if she thinks he's a bad boy."

"She likes bad boys?" Snow had to ask.

"All women do," Jade said. "Even girls like Emily."

"Okay, we need to try this on you," Liza bid him. "Bathroom's on the other side of the hall."

Snow changed out his jeans for the red Santa pants in that bathroom. He pulled off his cut and t-shirt, walking out the tidy little bathroom with Santa's coat slung over his arm. Before he could open the door to the room where Liza and Jade were waiting, he glanced back up the hall leading to the bakery's storefront. His gaze met with Emily's a split second before she vanished, blue eyes wide.

Snow chuckled. She'd gotten an eyeful of his scars, his tats. He hoped she liked what she saw.

Liza and Jade worked efficiently. The Santa suit fit him reasonably well. Liza didn't want to take the waist in too much because they'd need to pad him to fit the coat. Since the bakery closed at six and it was almost six-thirty, Snow hurried to change back into his own clothes. Emily would want to go home.

He handed the suit to Liza. Jade had already left, as he walked with her to the front of the bakery. He paused as the two of them walked out the door.

"Do we need to lock this?" he asked.

Before Liza could answer, he heard raised voices. And he was pretty sure one of them was Emily. When he dashed around the corner to see who else was there, he found Emily in a heated argument with some suit that looked familiar. The older man had her crowded against her SUV in a way Snow really didn't like even though the man wasn't much bigger than her.

"There a problem here?" Snow asked as he approached them.

Emily's face was flushed from the argument, her eyes wide on Snow as he stopped at her side.

The little man, in his little suit, stared up at Snow for a moment from behind glasses that were way too big for his face. It made the man's dark eyes smaller and meaner looking.

"I'm having a private conversation with Ms. Frost, if you don't mind," the man said as his gaze moved over Snow in a dismissive way. "If you'll excuse us."

Snow wasn't going anywhere.

"Not a conversation if there's yelling," Snow said. "And I heard you yelling at Ms. Frost."

Emily wasn't stopping him.

"This visit wouldn't be necessary if Ms. Frost would honor her commitments," the suit said to him. To her, he said, "I'll talk to you very soon."

They both watched the suit strut back to his car, his brand-new electric luxury car no less. The little bastard spun rocks out of the bakery parking lot.

Emily was shaking, leaning against her car.

"Are you okay?" he asked her, voice low.

Emily nodded, swallowed hard. Her trembling didn't ease. "I'm f-fine."

"The hell you are," Snow said. "Let's go back in the bakery for a minute, yeah?"

Guiding her back around to the door, Snow nodded to Liza as they passed her.

"I've got this," he told her.

Emily wrapped her arms around herself as she

walked, leading him to her office in the very back. A quick glance around showed him that it was as cheery and welcoming as the woman herself was. Still, she looked so small as she took a seat in the chair behind her desk.

Snow realized her putting her desk between them was a defensive mechanism. But it wasn't what she needed right now. He walked around the desk, taking a knee put him on eye level with her. And she was still shaking.

"Want to tell me what that was about?" Snow asked, gently.

Tears now, shining in her eyes and starting to spill. Snow felt a moment of panic. He was no damn good with tears no matter who shed them. It hit even worse that they were coming from a woman who worked so hard to appear strong and self-sufficient.

Snow expected some smart-ass answer but as she swiped at her eyes with her hands, she tried to smile. "Everything is fine, really. It's just a misunderstanding. I'll call the bank in the morning and straighten it out."

That's where he'd seen the suit before. Engle & Trust was the oldest bank in Mercy and more than a little shady.

"Why was he *here* shaking you down?" Snow wanted to know. "That's not an appropriate way to do business."

"I don't know," she said after a moment. "It took me off guard."

"Is the bakery struggling?" he asked.

Trying hard to pull herself together, Emily shook her head but didn't say anything. After a moment, she rose from the chair, and he rose with her.

Her smile didn't reach her eyes when she said, "I need to get home now. Thank you for your concern.

But I'm sure it's a misunderstanding. That's all."

Brave. Snow admired that about her.

He walked her out, neither of them saying anything. He didn't try to make her talk to him. Snow understood pride all too well. But until he knew what was going on, he was going to keep her safe. His bike was parked just behind her SUV, and he waited until she'd driven away before he fished his phone from his pocket.

Axel answered pretty quickly. "Yeah?"

"Didn't you make friends with one of the tellers at Engle & Trust?" Snow asked. He hoped he guessed correctly. It also could have been Axel's twin, Ryder.

"That was Ryder," Axel told him. "Why?"

"Where's Ryder? I have a situation," Snow said.

"The clubhouse," Axel said. "I'm heading that way myself."

"See you there in five minutes." Shoving his phone back in his pocket, Snow started his bike and headed in the direction of the clubhouse.

* * *

Emily

Once she made it home, Emily locked the door and hung up her coat. She made it to the kitchen, pouring herself a quick glass of wine as she focused on her breathing. She'd taken one drink from that glass before she burst into tears.

Emily felt so defeated.

Things had been slow at the bakery the last few months. She hadn't missed a single mortgage payment until this month. As of today, her payment was two weeks late. Emily understood being late paying for anything was bad. Fees were incurred, it was bad for her credit score. All of that, as much as she hated it, she understood.

But bankers didn't just show up at someone's business to confront people like that, did they? It had been mortifying to find the angry banker waiting at her SUV, yelling at her out in the open. Even worse, she had once dated the man's son.

She didn't need the entire town to know she was struggling.

If she'd been a man, would that have happened?

It was just the culmination of everything she'd been dealing with since Thanksgiving. Money was a constant struggle and no matter what goodies she sold or sales she offered, it wasn't moving the needle. She'd cut back on everything she could. She'd canceled all her streaming services; got a less expensive cell phone plan. She lived alone and tried to make cheap meals like chili or stew that she could eat for several days.

She was behind on her payments for the bakery for the first time. Her SUV needed repairing but she couldn't afford it. It was just as well she lived alone, because she couldn't afford Christmas. And the annual children's event? Their regular Santa Claus was unavailable and this year a really hot guy from a motorcycle gang was taking his place. If he did a bad job, she'd be blamed for that too and that would be just another strike for her business.

Emily just hoped that she was able to get caught up on her payments. They always held the annual children's event at her bakery. That was two weeks from now. Would she still have a bakery to host the event by then?

Stop. Stop.

Emily dried her tears and grabbed the lasagna she'd made Monday night, warming up one of the last two portions. Thinking about everything going wrong in her life wouldn't do any good.

She just needed to get to the bakery early tomorrow, come up with some more new holiday treats. Then she'd hit social media to try and drum up some business. Special treats for Saturday when people were out Christmas shopping and Sunday after everyone got out of church. Maybe she could make enough this weekend to make her payment and at least get through December.

She wouldn't even think about January right now, which was always scary slow. Not right now.

As she ate alone at her kitchen table, the wine taking a little of the edge off, she thought about the man, Ian's father, from back when they dated. The fact only made the incident all the more humiliating.

But Snow's voice ran through her mind.

Why was he here shaking you down?

It wasn't a bad question.

When she finished her lasagna, she put her dish in the sink. But her mind wasn't on it.

Elliott Kidd.

Emily had dated his son Ian a few years ago. She remembered him mentioning his father worked at a bank. The relationship hadn't ended well because Ian was controlling, and Emily wasn't willing to give up control of her life to anyone.

Like she was doing a great job on her own.

Ian had moved out of Mercy after stalking her for weeks after the breakup. Was he back? Did that have anything to do with his father confronting her in such a nasty way?

If he was willing to do that, would he try to take her bakery?

Emily finished her glass of wine and had another after that. But it didn't help her sleep. No, she lay awake for a long time with her worries preying on her mind. Her mind kept circling back around to a certain biker too.

Chapter Three

Snow

"You're doing fucking what?" Axel's brows shot up as Snow finished his beer. "Santa Claus?"

Snow grinned at Hero before cutting his gaze back to the twins, Axel and Ryder. "I'm playing Santa Claus for the kids' Christmas party they do each year. What's wrong with that?"

"Lame," Ryder said, shaking his head. "I get you have white hair, dude. But you're a little young to play Santa. And you don't have his figure."

"I'll take that as a compliment," Snow told them.

"How did you end up agreeing to that?" Ryder asked.

"Jade," Snow and Hero said in unison.

"Still lame," Ryder said as Razor, their club's prez walked into the room.

"Shut it," Razor said to the twins. "Or I'll tell Jade you two are interested in playing elves."

Axel put his hands up defensively. "I didn't say anything. Leave me out."

Razor winked at him. "That's what I thought you said."

"Jade's not the only reason he's doing it," Hero said, grinning.

"What's the other reason?" Razor asked.

"One cute little bakery owner." Hero winked at Snow.

"She is cute." Pulling out a chair, their prez joined them at the table. "What's up this evening, gentlemen?"

Snow knew it wasn't a direct question, but he was going to answer it that way.

"Does anyone know anything about Elliott

Kidd?" Snow threw it out there. "Branch manager of Engle & Trust?"

"Might," Razor said. "Why?"

Snow ran a hand over his lower face. It had been a while since he'd shaved his face, and he was still getting used to it. "He showed up at Emily's bakery earlier, shouting at her in the parking lot."

"Really?" Razor asked.

Snow nodded. "I get the impression she's behind on her bank loan."

"Yeah, but usually you get notices in the mail or a phone call," Axel said. "You usually don't have bank managers showing up at your place of business to yell at you."

"That is uncommon," Razor said. Turning to Hero, he said, "That one prospect. Perry? Isn't he dating a teller from that bank?"

"No," Hero told him. "It's Ryder."

"Ryder." Razor craned around to meet the gaze of Axel's twin brother. "You have a lady friend at the bank?"

"A couple," Ryder replied with a shit-eating grin.

"See if one of them can look into this?"

"Will do, prez," Ryder said.

"When's the kids' party?" Razor asked Snow.

"Friday after next," Snow said.

"Why did you shave your face?" Razor's gaze took him in. "Santa has a beard."

"Apparently, they're going to glue a beard on," Snow told him. "And they'll pad me up. I'm supposed to go back tomorrow to try the suit on again. Liza Austin is doing the adjustments."

"You going to the greenhouse?" Razor asked.

Snow shook his head. "The bakery."

Snow didn't miss the sly look exchanged

between Hero and Razor.

"I get why you signed up for this," Razor said. "But are you going to be able to pull that off? Are you any good with kids?"

Rolling his eyes, Snow met Razor's gaze. "You're not the first person who's asked me that. The answer is the same. I have a couple of nephews in Franklin County. I do okay with them."

"You have siblings?" Hero asked, looking surprised.

"I do," Snow told him. "Just one sister. And she's got two boys. I've spent some time with them. They're good kids."

"As long as you know what you're getting into," Razor told him, chuckling. "Until we find out what's going on with the banker, let's keep an eye on the baker's place. What's her name again? Emily Freeze?"

"Emily Frost," Snow corrected him.

"Where's she live?" Razor asked.

"Vinnie Street," Snow said without thinking.

Razor's expression was knowing. "You don't say. All right. That's only a couple of miles away from you and Jade, Hero. Ask Jade to help you keep an eye out. I'm sure Snow will too."

When his prez winked at him, Snow nodded. Until they figured out what the banker wanted, he appreciated the help keeping an eye on Emily. Axel had confirmed his own thought. Bankers didn't usually show up at a person's place of employment to confront them like that.

Was she in a lot of debt? Or was there something else going on? Snow didn't know Emily enough to pry. He wanted to. But at the moment, he had to settle for surveillance.

It was all about keeping the stubborn little baker

safe. Yeah, she wasn't sold on him as Santa Claus for the kids' event. Hell, she wasn't sold on him period. He just had to hope that maybe Jade and Liza were right. If all women liked "bad boys," just maybe he stood a chance with Emily.

"Anyone up for a game of poker?" Ryder asked. "Since we're here anyway."

"We have beer?" Razor asked, before committing to anything.

"There's a case in the fridge," Axel said.

"Bring me one," Razor called.

Snow stayed where he was as Ryder approached the table with a deck of cards to get their poker game started.

* * *

Emily

Emily's mind was spinning when she got off the phone with the woman calling from Mercy's elementary school. The principal of the school said the baker who usually helped them had a family emergency and the Christmas party they had each year at the school was on Thursday. Could she help them?

The baker the lady mentioned had to be Corrine Martens. While Emily visited Mercy before she opened her shop there, she hadn't immediately known about the woman who made specialty cakes and other treats out of her home. The lady was a native of Mercy and apparently had been taking orders for years.

Including from the school. Emily wrote everything down, all the items they wanted. A huge cake, boxes of cookies, and other treats. They wanted everything delivered to the school by noon on Thursday. Day after tomorrow. And it was almost closing time today.

Why did everything always go that way? She would have been overjoyed to get the order if there was more than 40 hours' notice. And if it wasn't the same week she need to make a shit ton of items for the children's Christmas party on Friday.

Still, if she did a good job, she could get more orders from the school.

No time to feel sorry for herself. It was an opportunity, and she was going to do the best job she could.

Shaking her head, she headed back to her pantry to make sure she had everything she needed for the order. Jotting down what she needed to pick up from the store, she was so lost to her task she didn't realize someone was in her bakery until she heard shuffling.

What now? It was ten minutes until closing time.

Snow stood on the other side of her counter, again looking over the baked goods she had left from the day. Without looking up, he said, "Can I get one of those Santa hat cupcakes?"

"Sure." Emily went to grab one from inside the case. "Is it to go?"

"Nah, I'll eat it here," he said. "Waiting on Liza and Jade. We're fitting the Santa outfit again for Friday."

Friday. The children's Christmas party. It was hard to keep her panic at bay at the reminder. Placing the cupcake and a napkin on a small tray, she slid it across the counter to him.

"Would you like anything else?" she asked, eager to get back to doing her quick inventory.

Now, he was looking in the small drink cooler next to her cash register. Pulling out a bottle of water, he placed it on the counter too. Before she could dash back to the pantry, she noticed he pulled out his wallet.

"That's not necessary," she told him. "It's on the house since you're helping us out with the kids' party. Remember?"

As if she hadn't said anything, he slid a ten-dollar bill across the counter. "I don't need any change," he said.

"Thank you," she said, tucking the bill into her cash drawer. "I hope you like it."

With that, she spun and went right back into the pantry, consumed with making sure she had everything she needed for the school order and the kids' Christmas party on Friday.

"Everything okay?"

Emily jumped, his voice coming out of nowhere scaring the shit out of her.

Snow was standing in the pantry's doorway, leaning to one side. "Sorry. Didn't mean to scare you."

"Everything's fine," she said. "Just doing a quick inventory for this week."

"Gotcha," Snow said. But he wasn't going anywhere. "Had any more trouble with your banker friend?"

That stopped her cold. It was mostly embarrassment that he heard any of that, but it also pricked at her anger.

"No." It was true. She hadn't seen Ian's father since last week. "And if it's okay with you, I'd rather not talk about it."

"Okay," Snow said. "I just didn't like how he spoke to you that day."

"Me either," she said. Stopping, she gazed up at him from where she crouched on the floor, looking over the contents of the bottom shelf. "I'm sorry. I really need to get this done. If you wouldn't mind waiting for Liza and Jade up front, I'd really appreciate it."

After a beat, she realized he wasn't going anywhere. When she returned her gaze to him, he was grinning. And she wasn't about to admit that grin made her feel things. Why did the annoying bastard have to be so handsome?

"What?"

"Need some help?" he asked.

"I appreciate the offer. It's just it would take me longer to explain what I'm doing than it would to just do it myself."

"It's inventory," he pointed out. "How hard can it be?"

Emily elected to ignore that. Maybe if she stopped talking, he'd get the hint and head back to the front.

Snow stayed right there, watching her work. After a moment, something occurred to her. He brought up Ian's father confronting her in the parking lot, paid for the cupcake and water, and now was offering to help and not really taking no for an answer.

After she finished that bottom shelf, she rose, her gaze locking with his. "Look, I really do appreciate that you want to help. I do. But I'm really okay. I just need to get a lot of things done between now and Friday for the Christmas party."

Confusion bled into his expression. "Do you get paid something for the Christmas party?"

"No, but I got another big order from the elementary school, and they want it by noon Thursday." Her anxiety shot up from just talking about it.

"You staying late to work on everything?"

Why was she having to explain to the biker *why* she was doing anything and when?

"Why do you want to know?" Emily asked, tired of the entire conversation.

"Because with the banker's behavior last week, I really don't think it's a good idea for you to be here alone, especially after hours."

Of course he would know the bank manager of the only bank in town. If not for the position she was in, she would have appreciated the concern. As it was, with two huge orders back-to-back, she didn't even have time to think about Ian or his father right now.

"Thank you," she said. "I'm not planning on working over tonight. Maybe tomorrow. Depending on how much I get done. But I'll be okay. Really."

That concern still showed on his face. "It's okay to ask for help when you need it."

"I would. But I don't." She led him back up to the front.

"I knew you'd say that," Snow said. "I don't know you that well, but I know that."

"What do you know?" Now she was pissed off. "You don't know anything about my orders or any other part of my life. Why would you be so worried for a stranger?"

"Because the manager of the local bank was in your parking lot yelling at you," he said.

When he put it like that, yeah, it was embarrassing. Then he'd insisted on paying for the cupcake and water.

"Like I said, I'm fine," she said, trying to glare him down.

"Okay, okay." Snow held up his hands in surrender. "I'm not trying to pry or butt in. But if you need anything, let me know. No strings attached. Honest."

Emily didn't know him well either, but the

sincerity in his voice, his expression, had her heart squeezing in her chest. He meant it.

"I'm sorry." Emily shook her head. "I'm not trying to be an ass. I'm just feeling overwhelmed between this week and everything else." She wasn't about to talk about her money problems. "I really do appreciate the offer."

"Even from a biker?"

Placing her list and pen on the counter, she folded her arms across her chest.

"I don't have a problem with you being a biker." She didn't. "I've just never really known any."

"Want to?" Snow grinned at her.

Why did that have her heart skipping a beat?

"Sorry I'm late!" Liza called out from the door. "Got stuck in traffic. Jade's on her way."

With the garment bag draped over one arm, Liza motioned for Snow to follow her to the back.

"Will you at least wait for us to do the fitting so I can walk out with you?"

If she did, she could finish her inventory in peace. Emily nodded. She headed back to the pantry to finish seeing what she needed. She heard Jade come in running back to join them, seeing if the newly altered suit would fit Snow.

Snow. What was his actual name?

Realizing it was closing time, Emily ran up to the front to put up her closed sign and lock the door. Looking around she didn't see anyone in the parking lot. With everyone occupied, she got back to her inventory.

* * *

Snow

"Well?" Snow turned slowly in a circle so the

two ladies working to fit him in the Santa Claus costume could see all angles.

Jade was nodding. Liza studied him.

"I think it's perfect," Liza said. "Outside of being younger, you look as good as Andy does each year."

He sure as hell hoped so. Liza had pretty much created a nylon belly stuffed with foam for him to wear under the suit. And it was realistic. It wasn't just sticking out the front like a pregnant belly. It also gave him side meat to complete the illusion.

Snow would have to give up the gym and pound beers for months to get the bod Liza gave him in just a few minutes. It had him chuckling.

He knew they were going to glue the beard on. What he didn't expect was the makeup.

"Is that really necessary?" he asked as Jade worked at putting rouge on his cheeks.

"His cheeks were like roses." Grinning, Jade stepped back, admiring her work.

"He's perfect," Liza said. "I think that's it."

"So what?" Snow asked. "I'll just be seated in a chair and kids are going to tell me what they want for Christmas?"

"Well," Liza said, walking a circle around him for one last check as he held the beard to his face. "Mostly. Some of the little ones might sit on your lap. Some of them might want to just stand there in front of you and tell you their Christmas wishes. And they get a picture with you."

"That works," Snow told her.

"In case I forgot to tell you," Jade said. "Thank you for doing this, Snow. We appreciate you. I know Emily really does. She was freaking out when Andy couldn't do this year."

"I'm glad to help out," Snow said. "Even though

I'm catching hell from the club. Totally worth it."

Snow took off the hat and handed it to Liza as Jade used a makeup wipe to clean off his cheeks.

"How many years you been holding this Christmas party?" he asked.

"This is our fifth year," Liza told him. "Emily is the one who started it."

Emily's idea. Somehow he wasn't surprised.

"That's nice. Kinda surprised that you have a single lady coming up with an event like that," Snow said. "Someone with no kids."

He didn't miss the look exchanged between Jade and the older woman.

"You'd think that. But if you know a little something about Emily's backstory, it makes sense," Liza said, unbuttoning the red and white coat he wore. "She moved here seven years ago, all by herself. She opened that bakery and she's just a little dynamo. A one-woman show. All of us were impressed."

Snow was impressed by her.

"She showed up at a town council meeting one day to propose the idea of a Christmas event for kids here in town, especially those that didn't have a lot. She wouldn't take no for an answer. I was the first person she recruited to help."

The pride in the older woman's voice had him smiling.

"We were putting together gifts that year for all the kids, just me and her." Liza put the coat aside and began to remove his Santa belly. "I just asked her, why she was so driven to put together an event like this. When she told me, it made complete sense."

"What did she say?" he asked.

"Her parents died on Christmas day." Liza lowered her voice. "She was in the car too, a baby. But she survived. The only family she had was her mother's parents and they raised her. They didn't have a lot. But Christmas hit hard every year for her, as you can imagine. Once she was grown, I think she decided that she wanted to do something for someone else for Christmas so she wouldn't have time to dwell on her own misfortunes."

Damn. That *was* a sad story. And partially explained why she was a loner when she could be married with kids of her own by now.

Once she'd pulled the belly off, he stood there in the white t-shirt they'd asked him to wear.

"She came up with the entire idea for the kids' party and some banker is over here yelling at her in her own parking lot?" Jade shook her head.

"Well, there's some history there too," Liza explained.

That got Snow's attention.

"When Emily first moved here, she started dating that banker's son, Ian," Liza went on. "But like his father, he's entitled and doesn't have the best manners."

"Really?" Snow asked. Now things were making a little more sense.

"Oh yeah," Liza told them. "The first party for the kids we had, Ian showed up drunk. Made a damn fool of himself in front of everyone there. She wasn't able to get him to leave and someone, one of the parents most likely, called the police. It was awful. Poor thing ended up in tears at the end of the night. She was convinced that there wouldn't be another one of these events in the future thanks to ole Ian."

Snow knew she must have been beside herself. But fortunately, Ian's dumb ass didn't end the event that first year.

"Ian still around?" Snow wanted to know. If he was, the MC would be keeping a special eye out for him.

"No, he left town not long after that," Liza said. "He shows up now and then to visit his family. He apparently always goes the extra mile to show up at the bakery with his latest girlfriend on his arm. All leggy, model types that look like they haven't eaten more than a salad since childhood."

What a jackass.

"I doubt any of them look half as good as Emily," Snow said before thinking about it.

Jade grinned. Liza nodded.

"You're right about that," Liza said. "Emily's just as pretty as a sunflower. Smart, has her own business. Nice person too. It's amazed me that some lucky fella hasn't snatched her up by now."

Working on it.

"Go get changed," Liza told him. "I imagine she's wanting to get home."

"Yeah, she's pretty stressed out," Snow told them. "Apparently, she got a big order from the elementary school for their Christmas party too."

That stopped Liza as she was packing up her sewing kit. "Corrine usually does those."

"Who's Corrine?" Jade asked.

"Uppity woman," Liza said. "Took a cake decorating class at the community college a while back and since then she thinks she's the bee's knees in baking."

"Is she any good?" Jade asked.

"Not really," Liza said. "It all looks nice, but it doesn't taste as good. True bakers, like Emily, can pull off appearance and taste. Good. Hope she gets more work then. She deserves it."

Snow could attest to Emily's baking skills. So far, what he'd sampled had been very good. And he wasn't the biggest fan of sweets.

Snow ducked into the bathroom to change back into his street clothes and when he made it back to the storefront, everyone, including Emily, looked ready to go. Liza and Emily asked them to be there early Friday evening to help set up.

Emily was in her SUV, backing out of her parking place. The sound it made caught Snow's attention as went to climb on his bike. Dashing to her SUV, he pecked on the driver's side window.

He could have laughed at the irritated expression on her pretty face. After a second, she put it in park, then powered down the window.

"You need to get this into the garage," he told her. "That grinding sound? That's your transmission."

He didn't like the way that irritation faded from her expression to be replaced by worry. "Okay. Thank you," she said.

"Axel could probably take a look at it for you," Snow said before she could put the window back up.

Emily sighed. "Let me get through Christmas. Then I might do that. Thank you."

Snow just hoped that SUV made it through the Christmas holiday.

Chapter Four

Emily

While she needed a good night's sleep to handle the next three days, worries preyed on her mind, keeping her awake. What if she couldn't pull off the school party? What if she did but didn't pull off the annual kids' Christmas party? What if she failed at all of it? Lost the bakery?

When she tried to take her mind off those troubles, a certain beautiful bastard of a biker haunted the few dreams she had. His smile, his gorgeous eyes. All the tattoos she'd seen on his upper body that first day he came for the Santa suit fitting.

Two cups of coffee got her out the door to the SUV. When she started it, she was immediately confronted with the noise Snow had pointed out. But at least it started.

Now, if I can just make it through the holidays.

Emily made it down her street, then the next. Right before she reached Route 221 that would take her into the heart of Mercy, the SUV just stopped accelerating. She coasted it to to a stop in the middle of the road. The engine was still running. Panic was a wild thing in her chest as she shifted into park. No trouble there. She shifted back into drive and gave it some gas. It wouldn't move. It was like being stuck in neutral.

When Emily shifted to reverse, yeah, it would move backwards. Another try shifting in drive? The SUV wouldn't move forward.

Fuck.

Now she was just stuck on a day she *really* needed to be there working.

Remembering Snow's offer of having his friend

look at it floated through her mind. She hadn't even asked for a number or the name of the garage if the friend even worked at one. Hell, she didn't have any way to contact Snow himself.

But Jade did.

Reaching for her purse in the passenger seat, she fished out her phone. Before she could find Jade's number, she noticed a truck coming to a stop behind her. *Great.* She powered down the window, using her arm to wave them around and threw on her emergency lights for good measure. When they didn't move, she huffed in annoyance.

Today's getting better and better.

When whoever was in the truck behind her climbed out, she knew a moment's panic and put her window up. Maybe she should call the sheriff's department. Whoever he was, he walked up to the side of her SUV and casually tapped on her window.

With her heart hammering in her chest, she lowered the window. The man who put himself on eye level with her outside the SUV was someone she didn't expect to see. It was her ex, Ian Savage.

"Emily," he said, same old smile on his face. "I'd forgotten you still lived in Mercy."

No, he hadn't. Fuck.

"Hi, Ian," she said, not holding his gaze.

"What's going on?" he asked, his breath pluming out on the cold morning air.

"I just called a towing service to come and get me." That was as close to the truth as he was going to get. "But thanks for checking on me."

"And they're on the way?" he asked, his dark-eyed gaze riveted on her.

"Yes," she assured him. "I'll be just fine. Thank you for stopping."

She pushed the button to raise the window when his hand on the window tried to halt its movement. She released the button on her door's panel.

"Come sit in the truck with me." It wasn't a request. "Keep warm until they get here."

Emily shrugged. "They'll be here any minute. There's really no need, Ian."

The sly smile she never liked formed on his face. "You don't want to catch up?"

That was the last thing she wanted.

"Thank you for the offer," she told him, again trying to put up the window.

Ian started pecking on the window again as she went back to her phone. Before she could select a number to call, someone was calling *her*.

"Hello?"

"It's Jade. Are you okay?" she asked. "We're here at the bakery."

"I'm fine." *Damn*. She was supposed to be meeting Jade with Emery first thing this morning. They were bringing chairs and tables from Sackett's for the kids' party on Friday. "I'm having a little car trouble, you know?"

"I'm sorry. Want me send someone to get you?" she offered.

"Yes, please," she said automatically. Anyone who could get her away from Ian. Snow's face flashed in her mind, his mention of her transmission that she had ignored running through her head.

Ian kept pecking on the window while she just tried to act like she didn't see or hear him. When his fist came down hard in the windshield in front of her, she yelped in fright.

"I'm talking to you, goddamn it!" Ian yelled. "Get out here! Now!"

It was a stark reminder of why she'd ended the relationship. Ian's anger and his tendency to be unreasonable when things didn't go exactly his way.

Now I remember.

Fighting the instinct to do what he wanted, and it wasn't easy, she tried to pretend to read her phone. When Ian marched back to his truck, she hoped it meant he was leaving. Trying to watch in her rearview mirror, she saw him climb up in the truck, and it looked like he was searching for something. Her hopes sank when he climbed back out.

Ian had a lug wrench in his hand.

Before she could dial 911 or he could do anything with that lug wrench, she heard the roar of a motorcycle. It came from 221, heading in her direction fast. The rider wasn't wearing a helmet, and the sight of his white hair had her heart racing in a good way.

It was Snow.

He parked the bike right in front of her SUV, climbing off quickly. But his attention wasn't on her. It was on Ian. Emily opened the window just enough to hear what was said.

"Hey, thanks for stopping by but everything's fine," Ian's tone changed to friendly with dizzying speed. "The tow truck is on its way. Thank you."

"Is it?" Snow nodded to the lug wrench in Ian's hand. "What are you planning to do with that?"

"It's not really your business, is it?" Ian's tone held a hint of warning. "I'll stay here with my girlfriend until the towing service gets here. You can move along."

"She's not your girlfriend." Snow took a step in his direction. He was taller than Ian, with wide shoulders and a menacing stance. "And I'm not going anywhere."

Ian took a step back and he looked really pissed off to be doing so. He shot an angry glare in her direction.

"So this is what you're doing these days?" Ian asked. "Slumming it?"

Before she could answer, Snow grabbed Ian by the front of his coat and slammed him back against his truck.

"You're not talking to *her* right now," Snow said. "You're talking to me. And you're going to go back to your truck and take your lug wrench with you before I shove it up your ass."

"You're threatening me?" Ian had no other card to play.

"Weren't you threatening *her*?" Snow asked. Yanking Ian away from the truck, he roughly shoved him away. Snow's expression had her believing he'd do just what he said if Ian didn't leave.

Snow stood there, glaring Ian down until he started the truck and carefully drove around them. Ian flipped Snow off as he made his exit. It wasn't until his truck was out of sight that Snow turned, and she opened the window for him.

"Let me guess," Snow said. "An ex?"

Emily nodded. "I'm sorry you had to deal with him."

"Not as sorry as I am that *you* had to deal with him." When he motioned her out of the SUV, she killed the engine and put the window back up before climbing out to join him. His gaze moved over her before he asked. "You okay?"

Emily nodded, shaking. She was grateful he'd arrived when he did.

"Hey." Snow pulled her into a hug, and she went with it. He was warm and solid. His arms felt like bands of steel wrapped around her. "You're okay."

"Thank you," Emily muttered into the coat he wore as he just held her there.

Another vehicle arrived. Snow moved his bike, and they watched the tow truck as it moved in front of Emily's SUV and backed up so they could hook it up. The man that climbed out of the truck had longer dark hair and he was nearly as big as Snow. Whoever he was, he smiled when he reached them, and that smile got her attention.

Where had all these attractive men been in the last six or so years in Mercy?

"Thanks, Ryder," Snow said, when he reached them. "This is Emily. Emily, this is Ryder. He and his brother own the garage in town. He's going to tow it back there to fix it."

She nodded, trying to fight back another wave of anxiety. She didn't have the money to rebuild her transmission. But she needed a car to get to the bakery and for deliveries. "Thank you so much," she told Ryder.

"You bet," he said.

"We need to get her to the bakery ASAP," Snow told him. "And she's probably not going to want to ride on the back of my bike."

While he was right, she realized she wouldn't mind trying it one day. Especially if she got to hold onto him for the ride.

"I would offer to drive her once I get this hooked up," Ryder said. "But we've got that covered too." A beat after he said that, Jade arrived in her SUV.

Emily's gaze met with Snow's. The thoughtfulness of how they handled the entire situation had tears stinging the backs of her eyes.

"Go with Jade," Snow told her. "You have a lot

going on. We'll handle this."

"Thank you," Emily told him.

Grabbing her things from her SUV, she scrambled to get in Jade's.

* * *

Snow

"Are you good, bro?" Axel asked as Snow stormed into the garage.

Snow was fuming. He needed to get himself in check before he hunted the son-of-a-bitch down.

So the shithead with the lug wrench was Emily's ex. The fucker had been in a rage outside Emily's SUV with a lug wrench in his hand. She'd been cowering in that SUV in a way that had Snow seeing pure fucking red.

"No," Snow said. "I'm pretty fucking far from being good. I need to figure out who the fuck that guy is."

"Ian Savage," Ryder said. "His father was the one who was yelling at her in her parking lot from what you said."

"Really?" Snow asked.

"What was he doing with the lug wrench?" Ryder looked confused. "The transmission was out, not a tire."

"That's a good fucking question," Snow said. "Especially with her looking terrified inside her vehicle."

Ryder shrugged. "Well, I haven't had a chance to look at it yet, but I'm guessing the transmission is shot. What do you want to do here?"

It was hard for Snow to push thoughts through his anger. But he needed to focus. Emily needed their help. He'd find that fucker and his lug wrench later.

"If you could rebuild that transmission, I'd be grateful, brother," Snow told him. "I'll pay you for it."

Ryder smiled. "You're paying, huh?"

Snow nodded.

"I bet you haven't even fucked her yet." Ryder crossed his arms over his chest.

"It ain't like that," Snow told him. "That little lady is having a tough time and I'm just trying to help."

Ryder's brows rose. "You're not in her league, brother. She's a well-to-do baker who is temporarily down on her luck. Once her luck has turned, you think she'll still be interested in you?"

"Hope so," Snow said. Especially since she hadn't asked him for anything. She wasn't playing him to get help. "We'll see how it goes."

"I just hope that cake isn't a little too rich for you," Ryder told him.

Snow understood his concern. His friend meant well. "Yeah, maybe it is. But I don't mind eating one from time to time."

Ryder laughed with him. "All right, I'll get on this."

"Take your time," Snow said. "She'll need a ride in the meantime and that means I'll get to spend some time with her."

"You think she's going to ride on the back of your bike?" Ryder asked.

He had a point. Plus, she needed a way to help her with deliveries. "Yeah, I should probably go home and get the Jeep. I've got time. Especially since I'm off until next year."

"Must be nice to do whatever computer shit you do for a living. I'd tell you that you could help with this, but you'd just be in my way."

That had Snow laughing. No, he wasn't the best mechanic. But it did give him an idea. He couldn't be of much help to Ryder, but there was someone he *could* help.

"Call me if you need anything," Snow told him as he headed for his bike.

On the ride back to his place, Snow remembered what Liza told him about Emily. The fact that she really had no family and worked so hard to do something for kids in the town for Christmas meant something to him. Maybe Liza was right in that she did it to take her mind off her own troubles. Still, it was a good cause, and he didn't mind helping.

Ryder wasn't wrong in what he said. Emily was way out of his league. But they had some things in common. Snow and his sister had been raised by a single mother and they'd seen plenty of hard times. If they had a party for kids like that when he was growing up, he might have hated going. Well, he would have acted like he did. But deep in his heart, yeah, he probably would have been grateful.

Parking the bike in the garage, he glanced over at his Jeep. He barely drove it. But today, it was going to come in very handy.

* * *

Emily

She was still shaken when they reached the bakery. Emery waited in his truck, all the tables and chairs in the back. He waved as they pulled into the parking lot.

Emily was so grateful for their help in setting up.

Jade parked, killed the engine. With a deep sigh, she turned to Emily. "Are you okay?"

"Yeah, I think so." *No.* "I'm just feeling

overwhelmed, you know? I've got the kids' party Friday. I got an order for the elementary school for their Christmas party."

"Oh, right," Jade said. "I heard Corrine had a family emergency and had to head up to West Virginia for the holidays."

Good ole Corrine. "My transmission is out. And yeah," Emily admitted.

Jade's look was sympathetic. "Everything happens all at once. Especially the bad stuff."

"Yeah, it really does." Emily tried to smile. "Thank you for helping with the Christmas party Friday. It means everything."

"I'm so happy to help."

Emily unlocked the bakery and the three of them worked at getting the tables and chairs out of Emery's truck bed. They carried them into the spare room that Emily rented out once in a while for a local book club and sometimes events for the local VFW. When they returned to the truck after a couple of rounds, Emily saw a black Jeep drive up, parking next to Jade. Who was that?

When Snow climbed out, Emily couldn't help but smile. "What are you doing here?" she asked when he reached them.

Snow didn't wait for an invitation to grab a table all by himself, and they were nice, heavy tables.

"Can you use some help?" he asked.

It's okay to ask for help.

"Yes," Emily replied. It wasn't nearly as hard to say that word as she always thought it would be.

Snow moved on with his table. Jade elbowed her, smiling.

Once they got all the tables and chairs in, Emery had to go. But Jade was able to stay long enough to help Snow set everything up while Emily got started on the baking. There was just so *much* to do. She had most of the treats for the bakery today in the ovens when Jade and Snow walked back into the store.

"Got everything arranged," Jade said. "Even got the tables covered for you."

It was that much less that she had to do. "Thank you both," Emily said. "I appreciate it more than you know."

"You're welcome," Jade told her. "I'm out of school at 3:30, and then I'll be back."

That was good news.

Jade left but Snow stayed where he was. "What am I doing next?"

"You mean it?" Emily just stared at him. Was he serious? Her handsome biker wanted to help her in the bakery. "I mean, you've done so much for me already with this morning and my SUV."

"Yeah, Ryder is taking a look at the SUV," Snow told her. "I went and got my Jeep so I can be your transportation for the next couple of days."

"You don't have to do that, you know," Emily told him.

"I want to."

"Have you ever baked?" Emily asked him.

Snow shrugged. "Not really. But I'm good at following instructions."

Chapter Five

Emily

It was dark outside when Emily declared them done. The cake was beautiful, all the other trays of cookies and treats turned out well. The best part had been spending the day with Snow, who was a surprisingly fast learner. He also didn't need to keep a conversation going at all times. She appreciated that.

When he undid the frilly pink apron he wore, she had to laugh. What would his fellow bikers think if they could see him now? Snow winked at her as Jade pulled on her coat.

"If that's everything, I'm going to head home," Jade told them. "School lets out after the Christmas party. After cleanup, I should probably be out at two. Want me to come back over?"

"I'd love that," Emily told her. "Thank you. I'm starting to think I -- we might be able to pull this off."

"We're definitely pulling this off," Jade said, heading for the door. "Night!"

And then it was just her and Snow.

"What's next?" he asked.

When he gazed at her like that, it was hard to think of anything.

"The stuff for the school is all done and ready to deliver tomorrow at noon," she said. "We can go home."

As Snow reached for his coat, she said, "Oh, I also need to take what's left from today to the homeless shelter. If that's okay."

Snow nodded. "That's cool. You do that once a week?"

"Every day I'm open," Emily explained. "Otherwise, it just gets thrown out."

She couldn't read Snow's expression but the intensity of it had her heart squeezing in her chest.

"Okay, we can run by the shelter to drop this off on one condition," he said.

"What?"

"Neither of us have really eaten all day," he said. "We're getting dinner after the shelter."

"That's fair," she told him.

With everything boxed up, they got in the Jeep and dropped off the leftovers at the shelter.

When they pulled into Sackett's, Snow turned off the engine, gazing at her from the driver's seat. "You've never been here?"

She shook her head. Bars were never her thing, and she didn't handle alcohol all that well.

"You know Emery," Snow explained. "And they have food here. Best burgers in town."

It didn't sound so bad.

"Fine," she said.

It was warm and smoky in the bar, alive with lots of people. At the center of the room was a dance floor with couples or groups of young women dancing in the colorful lights to the music. The bar wasn't far from there and tables where people drank and ate surrounded all of it. Emily saw a couple of folks she knew, a lot of bikers, and young people who were probably home for the holidays.

She followed Snow out of the area, into another room. The room wasn't as smoky and had better lighting. Mostly tables, with a pool table in the center of that room and a counter for ordering food.

"Find us a seat," Snow told her. "I'll get food."

Nodding, Emily turned to hunt for a free table and found one close to the pool table. She took a seat, appreciating the warmth of the room.

"Look who's here," someone said from behind her.

Turning, Emily spotted Ryder, pool cue in hand.

"Hi," she said.

Ryder was playing against another man who looked exactly like him, a twin. The other man's hair was longer and that was literally the only difference between them. There was a woman, a cute redhead, hanging on the arm of Ryder's brother and she looked to be a little drunk.

"Thank you for helping with the SUV," she told him.

"You're welcome," Ryder said. "It's going to need a transmission rebuild. Shouldn't take more than a week or so."

She hoped he couldn't read the panic welling up in her. What was she going to do? She couldn't pay for that.

"Hitting on my girl?" Snow said when he reached the table with a tray. Two beers, two nice-looking burgers and a huge order of fries.

His girl? Emily was really trying to keep that from going to her head.

Ryder smiled. "Nah, talking shop. I was telling her about the SUV."

Nodding, Snow took a seat across the table from her. Pointing to the other man playing pool, he said, "That's Ryder's brother, Axel."

Emily nodded. "And the woman?"

"Ms. Right Now?" Snow told her.

"The twins are in the MC with me," Snow told her. "The Hounds of Hell."

Drinking from her glass of beer, Emily laughed. "That's an ominous name."

"Damn straight," Snow said, grinning.

"You sure ran Ian off this morning," she told him as they ate.

"Tell me about that."

Emily sighed. "I'd just moved to Mercy when I met him. Ian was a nice-looking guy and I gave it a try, but it didn't take long for his temper to show. When I ended it, Ian didn't take it well. Before he moved, he bragged to everyone about getting some high-powered Wall Street job. But I always suspected he left town because of me."

"What happened this morning?" Snow asked. "Before I got there."

With a sigh, she told him. When she brought up the lug wrench, she watched angry color seeping up from Snow's collar. "Yeah, that pissed me off," he said.

"I was terrified. Sure, he always had a bad temper, but he'd never threatened me like that before."

"He won't do it again," he said. "I guaran-damn-tee that."

"I'm just hoping he's not living here again," Emily explained. "He's here every Christmas. Usually, he just shows up in the bakery, always with some new woman on his arm. Always well-groomed, rail thin, perfect. Like greyhounds or something."

That had Snow laughing. "Has he been to the bakery this time around?"

"No."

"Son-of-a-bitch tried to warn me off. Said he was your boyfriend." Snow blew out an exhale.

"I don't want to talk about him." It was the truth. "Tell me about you."

Finishing his first beer, Snow nodded. "Not a lot to tell. I was raised by a single mother, and I have a sister, a couple of nephews. We didn't have a lot, didn't have other family we could count on. But we made it."

Emily could relate.

"How did you become a biker?" she asked, watching a smile transform his face.

"How did I *become* a biker?"

"Yeah. I know nothing about it. How did you get into all of it?"

"I've always loved motorcycles," he said, his expression shifting with the topic that was obviously important to him. "I had friends who were into bikes too. Some older guys in town had a club going, the Hounds. When we were old enough, we signed up as prospects. I patched in when I was twenty-one. I've been there ever since."

"How long is that?" she asked. "Your hair is white, but your face is young. It throws me off."

Snow chuckled. "I've heard that before. I've been in the MC almost fifteen years. Does that make me too old?"

Finishing her beer, Emily shook her head. "No. I'm almost thirty."

"Need another?" Snow asked. That smile of his had her head spinning as much as the beer.

"Yes."

They talked and drank. Snow told stories about the twins, who stayed around their table, telling stories about Snow that had her cackling. Emily was happy to listen, nursing the second beer he brought her. She had a nice beer buzz but still had her wits about her.

"Shit," Snow said when she was about to nod off, watching the twins face off in pool. "It's midnight."

Shit was right. She had to be at the bakery early tomorrow. They had to deliver the order to the school and get everything made for the Christmas party finished for Friday for the kids.

Saying their goodbyes, they made it back to the Jeep and they were in her driveway in the blink of an eye.

"You okay?" Snow asked, looking concerned and blurry.

"Yep, I'm fine," she said. "Just need to get to bed."

Snow nodded, looking so handsome in the dim light of the Jeep.

"Well, goodnight," she told him. And it was meant to mark her exit. She went to kiss his cheek. That's all. But somehow that kiss landed on his lips. Then he was kissing her back. And he was such a good kisser…

* * *

Emily couldn't say she knew exactly how they ended up in her house, in her bedroom. But she liked it. She liked the way Snow held her close, lowering her to her bed. When he paused to pull off his coat and shirt, she loved the collection of tattoos that were scattered across his skin. She wanted to trace each one with her fingers, her tongue. Beautiful images and words were layered on his skin with dark ink in shades of black and blue.

Emily rolled him under her, and he allowed it. She was gasping, grinding against him trying to satisfy a deep ache that she'd neglected for so long. Her hands slid up around his neck, her fingers sliding up into the white locks of his hair.

Snow's mouth painted the tender flesh of her neck with demand. One hand slid slowly up from her hip, plucking at the buttons of the sweater she wore.

"You sure about this?" Pulling back to look at her his gray eyes were storm dark now. "I'm always up for a good fuck but you're a little more than that for me."

Emily's heart raced at those words. She pulled one huge hand over her breast, and he squeezed her gently. It had been so long since she'd had a good fuck. At the moment, with the huge biker in her bed, she understood why. She'd always attracted either older men or nerdy types. They were nice men, some of them good looking. But not one of them had her feeling like this. She pressed herself against his palm, her pussy aching in a way that was raw and urgent.

"Let's start with that fuck, Snow," she muttered breathlessly as he tugged her sweater off and pulled down her bra to reveal her breast.

When he got his mouth on her, his tongue dancing around her nipple, she gasped, fingers clutching in his hair. He stopped abruptly. The hooks of her bra gave way as he ripped that away from her too.

"You're beautiful," he whispered, sitting up to lean against the headboard, keeping her draped across his lap.

With an iron-hard arm wrapped around her back to hold her in place, Snow teased both breasts with his mouth, teasing her into a frenzy. One large hand framed one breast while his lips played with the other. She learned fast that he liked her to pull on the silk of his hair, rewarding her with a deep moan around her nipple when she did.

He plucked at the front of her jeans, yanking at the zipper impatiently before sliding one big hand down the front, into the wet heat of her panties.

She was panting for him now. "Snow, please…"

The dirty smirk took her off guard.

"You feel so good." One rough fingertip traced the lightest circles around her clit, had every inch of her in flames. "But I want more."

Emily landed on her back the next beat, crying out in surprise. Snow tossed away her slides, peeled off her jeans with impressive speed. When her brain caught up, she watched Snow push her thighs apart, pressing a heated kiss to the inside of one knee.

Her fingers dug into the bedding beneath her, anticipation rippling through her body as his mouth blazed a trail up the inside of one thigh. Swipes of his tongue on her skin layered with careful nips of his teeth had her writhing before of him, rolling her hips in an effort to him where she wanted him faster. It had been *so* long.

After a moment, the beautiful bastard stopped and smiled at her. "I love how desperate you are," he whispered. "But you're not rushing me, Emmy. You're not the only one who's been waiting for this."

Her thighs were trembling as he continued to drop kisses on her skin, reaching her heated center. Snow nudged her covered mound with his nose gently before his hands slid up to grab her panties and peel them off. His gaze met hers as he pushed her thighs wider, spreading her bare petals apart. The scent of need rose on her body heat, and she couldn't bring herself to be embarrassed. Now with Snow smiling as he lowered his head, his lips innocently pressing to her outer lips first, butterfly kisses to swollen needy flesh.

When he dove in, it took her breath away. He kissed her pussy like he would her mouth, a dirty kiss that was all lips and tongue. Snow had her dancing on the tip of his tongue as he slowly worked one, then two of his large fingers into her. The stretch wasn't much, the burn slight. His fingers slid in and out of her so easily on the slick of her need.

Emily shook on the bed, her back arched, her fingers plucking at her nipples. She needed relief in the worst way. Snow's gaze was on her as he took her apart with the devilish tease of his tongue, the scissoring slide of his fingers inside her.

"You're being so good, Emmy," he whispered into her. "Taking my fingers so well."

When he eased a third finger inside her, the stretch almost brought her off as her body stretched around the intrusion. Need clawed at her core, had her tightening against the sensual onslaught. Whatever he was doing with his tongue on her clit was making her crazy. When his fingers curled up against her front wall, she wailed.

Snow doubled down then, knowing she was about to blow apart. His tongue twisted in her folds, one rough finger pad stroked within her until the edges of her world started to fade to black. When her orgasm slammed through her, she thrashed and cried out in his hold. Her hands clawed at the bed, pawed at his head.

Swiping at the juices shining on his mouth with the back of his hand, Snow rose over her. It wasn't lost on her that he was still had his jeans on while she was naked and shattered, sprawled over the bed.

Snow paused, reaching to turn on the lamp on her bedside table. With surprising care, he lifted her and placed her on the center of the bed. But Emily was past wanting careful or sweet. She wanted Snow to fuck her like there was no tomorrow.

The view of him shirtless in the light had her drooling. He had scars aplenty, faded silvery lines hidden in the landscape of ink he wore. But they did nothing to diminish the beauty of his powerful upper body.

Emily slid a hand down her body, her fingers trying to quell the ache, the emptiness he left her with.

Snow's eyes were riveted to her movements, watching and licking his lips as she worked her own fingers into her aching body. Standing, he toed off his shoes, worked off his jeans and boxers.

Snow without clothes was a goddamn masterpiece. Perfect abs, slim hips. His thighs were heavily muscled and powerful. She watched as he took himself in hand, stroking his swollen cock in a smooth motion as she marveled at its size.

Damn.

All she could do was stare, fucking herself on her own fingers. But her efforts were a poor substitute for Snow's touch. His knowing look told her he knew it too.

Snow climbed on the bed, batting her hands away and slotting himself between her quivering thighs, holding himself up on one arm. He pressed the swollen head of his cock into her wetness, sliding it gently up and down through her folds. Emily shivered in need, chewing her bottom lip and bracing herself.

Snow paused, his breath coming fast, and his handsome face flushed. "You ready for me, beautiful?"

"Please," was all she could mumble.

Snow pushed into her and she sucked in a breath. His heated length was wide and hard, splitting her open as he carefully sank into her. One big hand settled over her tummy as he claimed her, his thumb tenderly stroking over her clit to help ease the burn.

The fullness, the heat was everything. His heavy cock was the cure for the ache he'd inflicted on her, and she focused on breathing as he filled her.

Snow's gaze was fixed on the place where their bodies joined, groaning when he was fully sheathed in her heat. His eyes slid closed, his exhaling a sound of pure bliss. With a whisper of her name, Snow gently ground into her.

Emily's body pulsed in need. She needed him to move...

His gaze was heated on her, his breath fanning against her face. Snow lowered himself over her to claim her mouth in a careful kiss.

"Are you okay?" he whispered against her lips.

"Yes," she managed, gasping when he slowly slid out of her. The sting took her off guard. She'd never been with someone his size before. When he pushed back in, her walls gripped him and she rolled her hips, needing him deeper. Needing more...

Snow's strokes were careful at first, slow. "It's all I can do not to come right now," he whispered. "You're taking my cock so well. So fucking tight."

His large hand slid down her body, spanning her tummy. Snow moaned as he lightly pressed his hand there, his thrusts speeding up just a little.

"I can feel me in there," Snow's voice was low, rough. "Feel that?"

"Snow, please. I need you."

The pride and desire that flared in his eyes made her shiver. His heavy thighs pushed hers wider and his thumb carefully worked the center of her pleasure. His thrusts came faster, harder. Still, he was careful, holding back as he moved in her, stuffing her full.

Emily just held on for dear life, her fingers sliding on all those muscles. Her thighs locked around his hips as he moved, plunging in and out of her and hitting spaces inside her that she didn't know she had. Emily disappeared under Snow, but he kept his weight from her, loving her with lusty kisses as his lower body powered into her.

"Not going to last long," he whispered hotly in your ear. "You feel too damn good... Need you to come."

Snow's hand shifted on her tummy, his thumb teasing her clit. The weight of his hand changed how he felt when slid back into her, the point he hit with the next thrust making her cry out.

His kiss was deep and taming as he fucked Emily faster, hitting the same mark over and over. She shook, she begged. Her nails carved down his back until she exploded, her pussy clamping around him and pulsing as the powerful release turned her inside out. Her bedroom spun away, her cries and his blending into one ecstatic chorus as he reached his release inside her, working himself through it.

When Emily came back down, Snow was all she could see in her sleepy vision. He reached across her to turn off the lamp before spooning behind her, his warm body feeling so good behind her.

"Not the best time to ask," he said, still breathing fast. "But are you on birth control or..."

Emily's eyes slid closed, but she was smiling. "I've got an IUD." And she was really fucking grateful for it just now.

"Go to sleep, Emmy," he whispered in her ear.

She didn't need to be told twice.

Chapter Six

Emily

The principal of Mercy Elementary School was tall with an intimidating demeanor, but not unfriendly. When Emily and Snow arrived with the delivery for the school's Christmas party, Mrs. Jansing directed them to use the entrance at the back of the school and showed them to the cafeteria where the party would take place.

Once she and Snow had everything set up and ready for the party, the principal returned to the cafeteria, her stern gaze taking in their work. Emily was sweating bullets. Snow stood behind her, his hand capturing hers in support.

"Corrine has been the one doing our Christmas parties for years," Mrs. Jansing told them as Emily sent up every prayer she knew that her work would earn approval.

What if what she put together was lacking when compared to Corrine's?

"I'm disappointed," the woman said. "In all that time, she brought a couple of decent sized sheet cakes. The same oatmeal and chocolate chip cookies. A couple of pans of fudge."

Emily's heart started hammering. Fudge? She didn't remember fudge. Had she fucked up?

Snow's hand squeezed hers.

The woman's gaze moved over the three-tiered cake that honestly, Emily was rather proud of. A pretty white tower of cake that she'd decorated modestly, with red and green frosting as accents to complete the look.

"The cake looks incredible." The principal smiled. "All of it does. And there's more than enough for everyone, which has been a problem in the past. Now we'll have extras to send home with those who need it. Thank you."

Emily knew she was probably staring at the woman, but it couldn't be helped. Relief and pride washed over her at having pulled the last-minute order off.

"Thank you," Emily said.

Once they were back in Snow's Jeep, Emily let reality sink in. She had a generous check in hand, and they were on their way back to the bakery. There was a lot to be done for the kids' party tomorrow.

"See what happens when you let people help you?" Snow said as he started the Jeep.

"This just might be enough to catch me up on the loan," she told him. "Now if we can just make it through tomorrow."

"We'll make it."

Emily was ready to hop out of the Jeep as soon as they reached the bakery but Snow's hand on her knee stayed her. He leaned in to steal a kiss, a seeking kiss that reminded her of last night. And she was still reeling from that, sore in unusual places.

"Ready for round two?" she asked him when the kiss ended.

"Right now?" Snow chuckled. "Don't we have all the baking for tomorrow?"

Snow's mind went straight for the gutter. Emily laughed. "The baking is what I was talking about."

"Worth a try," Snow told her before they headed in.

* * *

Snow

"Is that it, Emmy?" he asked.

Snow didn't think he would ever get tired of the little smile that formed on her lips when he called her that. Yeah, she looked tired and that was partly his fault. But her eyes were shining bright as her gaze moved over everything they prepared for the kids' Christmas party tomorrow.

Well, *she* prepared. He helped but it was mostly grunt work. It was totally worth it to watch her work, to spend that time with her.

"I think so," Emily said.

Today had been the first time she didn't appear to be carrying the world on her shoulders. Her shoulders weren't hovering around her ears, the tense lines around her eyes were gone. His Emmy was beautiful and a little more relaxed, she was endlessly gorgeous to him.

The bakery had closed an hour ago and Jade had just left. He'd been ready if they'd ended up working all night on everything. It was a pleasant surprise that they were done and closing down the bakery for the night.

"Want to grab dinner?" she asked, pulling on her coat.

"Let's have something delivered."

Once they were in the Jeep on the way to her house, Snow watched her out of the corner of his eye. "Feeling better about things?"

"I am," she told him. "The check from the school will definitely help."

"Is the bakery doing all right?" Snow asked carefully.

That earned him a deep sigh. "Business has been slow this year. Normally, things are way busier between Thanksgiving and Christmas. I'm a little behind on my loan. But if I can keep my head above water, I've only got five more years and it's mine."

He was impressed. It was no small thing that a young woman like her had her own business, almost free and clear.

"And I really appreciate your help," Emily said. "And your friends. I haven't figured out how I'm going to pay for a new transmission, but I'll find a way."

And just like that, the tension and worry were creeping back in. He could have kicked himself for bringing it back with his stupid ass question. "I'll work something out with Axel and Ryder so you pay them back as you can," he said. "Is that better?"

She nodded, but he could tell she didn't like that answer. Emily was quiet until they got to her house. Once they were in the living room, Emily turning on the lights, Snow couldn't take the quiet anymore. "Did I say something wrong?" He wanted to know.

A deep sigh. "No, you didn't," Emily said. "Sorry, guess I'm just tired from the last couple of days."

"No, you're deflecting." Snow called her on it. "Why is it so hard to let other people help you out?"

That stopped her. Sinking onto her couch, she studied him. "Because for most of my life I was the only person I could count on."

Snow remembered the story Liza told him about her past, using that to frame what he wanted to say. "That's been true for your life up until now. But now you have people you can count on. Liza, Jade, and me." The intensity of her gaze almost forced his away. "Think about it," Snow said. "Think about this week."

"I know, Snow. I don't mean to sound ungrateful."

"I'm not looking for gratitude, Emmy," he told

her. "I'm just pointing out that you let me help you the last two days. You let Jade help and the impression I got was that it was her first time too. See how well everything went?"

Emily nodded, a tear spilling from one eye.

"We got to the school today and the principal was very happy with your work," Snow went on. "I'm not trying to take credit or give it to Jade. I'm just talking about you. See how much better things go when you let help in?"

"You don't think I could have pulled it off by myself?" she asked.

"Yes, I do," he said. "But it was a lot less traumatic, wasn't it?"

Emily couldn't say anything there. She had to know he was right. But why did she look so miserable? Taking a knee in front of her, Snow got on eye level with her. "What's wrong?"

She dropped her head. "I appreciate all the help, Snow. It's just... I guess I'm not used to having people be there for me, you know? Not for long anyway."

Based on what Liza told him, he could understand that. But he didn't think it all came from her childhood.

"I haven't had a lot of luck with relationships," she admitted. "Ian was the longest relationship I've ever had, and that wasn't even a year."

Given what a prick that guy was, Snow was surprised it'd lasted that long. "What happened there?" he asked.

That had her meeting his gaze. Swiping away the tear that escaped, she seemed to be weighing her words. "It started well," she said. "They always do. And at first, I really liked his possessiveness. I don't really have a family now and his family welcomed me.

It was nice. But the pleasantness didn't last long."

Moving, Snow sat next to her on the couch, taking her hand in his.

"Then I kept making mistakes with them. His family acted like I should automatically know what they wanted. How to act and what to do. His father wasn't so bad. Ian was controlling and jealous. His mother just encouraged his behavior." Emily shook her head. "By the time he and his mother decided we should get married, I was scared to death. I didn't have family or any close friends of mine to compare notes with. I just panicked. When I ended it, he stalked me for months. I ran into his mother at the grocery store, and she created a scene. They would come to the bakery, but I finally put a restraining order on Ian and his mother. For that, I'm the biggest bitch in the world."

Snow shook his head. It was all making sense now. The one time she let someone in, they betrayed her trust and mistreated her. "Not everyone is like him. Like them."

"I know," she told him. "I was younger and stupid. He was the son of a wealthy banker. He worked at an architectural firm, dressed well, had a nice car. I told myself that's the type of person I needed to look for. To be with. You on the other hand…"

"Didn't think a biker could be your type?" he asked.

Color darkened her face. "I don't know much of anything about bikers. I was a little scared. But you're nothing like him. I like the way you've treated me. I like the way you look." She snorted. "I don't know your real name. I don't even know what you do for a living."

Snow chuckled, holding out his hand. "August

Crowe. I work in Internet security."

Emily hadn't expected that. But the surprise faded quickly, and she leaned into him, wrapping her arms around him. Without words, his Emmy was saying she trusted him. And that was good enough for him.

"Hey, why don't you get ready for bed?" Snow told her. "Is it okay if I stay over?"

That earned him a smile that he considered just his. "Yes," she said.

"I'll have a pizza delivered," Snow told her. He turned out the lights in the living room as he called his favorite pizza place to place an order. Lights outside caught his attention and as he gazed out the window from the darkness of her living room, he saw the bastard's truck, creeping by her house. Probably because her car wasn't there but his Jeep was.

Ian. Snow was going to fuck him up. And he'd enjoy it. But at the moment, he had a bad feeling Ian was waiting for the worst time to fuck with Emmy. The children's party tomorrow at her bakery. Quick as he could, he fired off a text to Razor and Hero, asking for backup.

By the time he did all that, he found her in her bedroom. Her pajamas were cute as hell, the lights were low. There, with her hair a little messy and no makeup on, she was beautiful. As he walked into the bedroom, she smiled at him.

It was a smile a man would fight for.

"It's going to be an hour before the pizza gets here," he said, pulling off his boots. "They must be running behind."

Snow climbed up on the bed with her, tossing his cut and flannel as he did. Grabbing the remote, she stretched out on her side facing the TV, scrolling through channels to find something to watch. Once she found what she wanted, he grinned. "The Great British Baking Show, huh?" he teased.

His Emmy could watch whatever she wanted. Playfully, he pushed her onto her stomach, straddling her thighs as he slid his hands under her pajama top, his fingers finding her muscles tense. He grinned as he got to work, watched her fold her arms to cradle her head.

Emily hummed contentedly under his hands. Her skin was warm velvet under his fingers, the tension gradually eased from her as he worked. "That's it," Snow whispered. "Relax."

Her eyes were closed, the slightest smile on her lips. His hands slid over her lower back, down to the globes of her ass. The thin pajama pants weren't really much of a barrier.

"That feels nice," she said, eyes still shut.

Emily helped him when he went to peel down the bottoms. She took a deep breath as he moved down her body, allowing him to get his hands on the backs of her thighs. Snow worked that supple flesh. When he slid his hands back up, he could feel the damp heat near her center.

Gripping the hem of her top, Snow pulled it up and off her. Grinning as she shivered beneath him. She wouldn't be cold for long.

Snow smoothed his hands over her back, down her sides. She shivered again but for a different reason. Sliding his hands under her, he palmed her breasts. The centers were already hard little buds from his touch. Draping himself over her, he teased her ear with his lips. "Can I have you?" he asked gently. "Before the pizza gets here?"

Emily rolled her hips, a gentle grind into his

aching cock. As an answer, it would do. Snow chained heated kisses over her shoulder, down her back. He took his time, loving the way her fingers dug into the bedding, the restless little shifts of her body under his. When he reached those sheer pink panties, he lifted only long enough to yank them off.

His gaze met hers when she glanced at him over her shoulder, just in time to watch him grab a pillow from the top of the bed and stuff it under her hips. Her mouth formed a little "O" as he pushed her thighs apart, wrapped his arms around them. It just made him harder for her.

Snow loved the way she struggled in his grip as he took her apart with his mouth. He teased her lower lips, her weeping entrance, not even going where she desperately needed him yet. The tension in her thighs, the grind of her pussy against his mouth had his dick growing even harder. His Emmy was tangy as summer lemonade and Snow took his time, had her moaning before he even got to her clit.

By the time he was drawing on that pearl with the tip of his tongue, Emily came for him. Cried out for him. She was a responsive little thing and what man didn't appreciate that? Snow kept her there, worrying that little button with his mouth and enjoying the way her entire body lit up.

His name was whimper when he brought her off a second time, left her panting. Undoing his slacks, Snow took himself in hand. He was so hard it hurt. Pressing inside her, he had to close his eyes, to breathe through it. She felt so fucking good. So tight and soft around him. She had him fighting like hell not to come.

Once he'd worked his way into her as far as he could go, Snow eased himself over her, caging her to the bed. When he began to move, her sigh was contentment. Hell, her walls were still trembling around him.

"You feel good?" Snow slid his hands over hers, lacing their fingers.

"Yes," she whispered, her silken walls clamping around him making him groan, urging him to keep moving.

It was so easy to get lost in the feel of being inside her, being joined with her. She fit against him perfectly, her snug little channel able to take him. But the squeeze? *Fuck.* It was satisfying. Snow dropped enough of his weight on her to hold her in place as his hips worked, grinding into her over and over.

"You like this?" he whispered hotly in her ear, fucking her gently.

"Yes." It sounded like a plea. A plea for more? He'd give her more.

Snow held her to the bed and fucked into her, knowing the minute when the tension began building in her again. When her thighs tightened, Snow shifted, pushing them together and holding them tight with his own. Oh, it had her tight little passage clamping around him like a vise, and almost brought him off. But the position made it feel like a deeper plunge into her, gave him the angle he needed to hit the mark that would drive her crazy.

"Oh." The breathy little sighs she released sped up and her grip on his fingers almost hurt.

She struggled as the pleasure built, and he wanted her to. Snow wouldn't grant her a reprieve, wouldn't let up. Not until she came screaming one final time and she did, the sound echoing in the quiet of her bedroom. The flutter of her walls around him triggered his own release and he thrust into her hard and fast, unloading into her as currents of pleasure coursed through him, shook him like a storm.

Rolling onto his back, Snow struggled to breathe. That had been good. That had been so fucking good.

His Emmy was shaking when she lifted up onto her elbows, looking wrecked, looking fucking beautiful. Wrecked because of him. *He* did that.

"Hey." Snow traced a finger over her lower lip. "Want to take a nap until pizza time?"

At her nod, Snow pulled her to him for a kiss. He loved the tender feel of her lips against his, the way she submitted to him.

Helping her climb up the bed, he tucked her under the covers. She was blinking like a sleepy owl by the time he climbed off the bed to pull his jeans back on. Hopefully their pizza would be there soon.

Another night in her bed was something he very much wanted. Watching her drift off to sleep, Snow smiled. He couldn't remember the last time he felt anything close to the contentment he felt in that moment.

Chapter Seven

Emily

The sun was shining brightly the day of Mercy's annual children's Christmas party.

"Looks like we're ready," Myra said.

And they definitely were. Liza had just finished decorating the Christmas tree and the wreath she made for the door was beautiful. Myra had stuffed stockings that had each child's name on them, placed them on the table within easy reach of Santa's chair and helper. All the treats were ready and arranged artfully around the huge Christmas cake Emily always made. The chairs were set out for the parents. The photographer had arrived and was setting up.

Families would start arriving soon, so Emily ducked into the bathroom to change into her elf costume. It was the same one she wore each year, a cute green dress with a scooped neck and long sleeves, the cuffs trimmed in white. She had an elf hat that matched, and she situated it on top of her head. With the tights and ankle boots completing the look, she was ready to be Santa's helper.

Santa came in from the back of her shop. Liza had him in the suit, all the stuffing to make him round and jolly in place. His hat was in his hand and the only thing he needed now was the beard. But he stopped cold when he saw her.

"You didn't tell me you were Santa's elf." Snow grinned, outright ogling her. "When are you sitting on Santa's lap, little girl?"

Snow caged her to the wall, his lips teasing her neck as she giggled.

"Behave, Santa," Liza's said from behind them. "We still need to glue the beard on."

"Ugh," Snow said grinning. "This is going to hurt, isn't it?"

"Might when we remove it," Liza told him with a wink.

The first guests started arriving a few minutes after that. Everyone was in place. Emery greeted everyone and directed traffic, Jade and Liza were managing the treat table. Myra was busy rehearsing the little speech she did each year. Hero was sticking around, and he was with Jade, so she appreciated the help. When she saw the twins walk in from the back she waved. She didn't know they'd be here, but they were certainly welcome.

When it was time, Myra gave her speech. There were so many people there the twins were helping Hero bring in more chairs. And while everyone got treats and talked, Emily went back to her office to get Snow.

"Are you ready?" she asked.

Snow nodded, rising from her office chair. His eyes were on her as he came toward her. She laughed when his fingers toyed with the skirt of her costume.

"Not now, Santa," she said. "Later."

"Promise?" Snow bent to kiss her, the whiskers of his beard tickling her.

Santa got a round of applause when they walked into the room. Some of the adults were eyeing Snow hard because they knew it wasn't Andy. They were trying to figure out who was under there.

Taking her place at his side, Emily smiled as Santa greeted each child. Snow was a little formal at first, but it didn't take him long, especially with the smaller kids, to get into character. When it came to the older kids, Snow did even better with them. He was playing more of a hip Santa than the classic one Andy always presented.

They were maybe halfway through the line when Emily spotted him. Ian walked through the door, making his way through the flow of traffic into the room, his gaze fixed on her. Panic gripped her as she wondered what he was doing there. Did he really need to create a scene now? Here in front of all these people?

Her hands were shaking so badly that she dropped the next stocking she gave to Santa. His concerned gaze met hers. Then he smiled.

"It's okay," he said in a low voice. "He's not going to do anything."

No sooner had he said that Hero marched from where he stood at the back of the room in Ian's direction. The twins made it to him first. There was enough noise in the room that not many people even noticed the twins each taking one of Ian's arms and forcing him out of the room. Hero followed them.

"Trust me," Snow said, before smiling at the next kid in line.

It took another hour to get through the line, get everyone's picture, and then Santa himself thanked everyone for coming, wished them a happy holiday season, and told them he'd see them next year. Myra and Liza looked impressed. Jade winked at her.

Despite everything, they'd pulled it off. The charity event went smoothly. When the last candy canes were handed out and all their guests made it out the door, Emily sighed in relief.

"How are you holding up, Emmy?" Snow said close to her ear.

She turned and hugged him hard. She just had to. He'd been such an important part of the success of their event.

"Liza!" Snow called. "Can you come get this

beard off for me?"

"Sure, let me get the remover," she said, heading to the back for her bag.

"That anxious to get out of the beard?" Emily asked.

He chuckled. "It does itch."

Once Liza removed it, Snow smiled and kissed Emily soundly. "Is it okay if I cut out?"

Snow wasn't just asking Emily but Jade, Liza and Myra.

"Yeah," Emily told him. "We've got this."

Snow nodded, the smile fading. "I've got to go take care of something."

Emily shivered, tugging at the skirt of her costume. "Did Ian --"

"Don't you worry about a thing," Snow told her. "I won't be gone long. Stay with Jade."

Jade was right there as Snow marched from the room. Emily watched him leave, feeling uneasy.

"Jade, do you --"

"Everything's fine." Jade smiled. "Let's get this mess dealt with. Then we can have some wine."

"Now that's a plan," Liza said, already gathering discarded plates and napkins.

* * *

Snow

As they'd agreed to over text, Hero and the twins took Ian the shithead back to the garage where they all worked. Snow didn't even bother to take off the Santa suit as he climbed from the Jeep and made his way to the back.

The three of them were there, waiting for him. Ian was duct-taped to a chair, a black sack over his head. The fucker was shouting obscenities, threatening to have them all arrested, to sue. Hero looked relieved when Snow reached them.

"Thank fuck," Hero said. "This is one really fucking annoying."

"You're going to think I'm fucking annoying when you're thrown in jail!" Ian yelled. "All you low-life motorcycle fucks can kiss my ass. Don't know you know who I am?"

Snow roughly grabbed the sack and pulled it off his head. Ian's face was red, his eyes glassy. Had the fucker been crying? He glared up at Snow, his smile a cruel line that didn't reach his eyes.

"There he is," Ian said. "Emily's really dropped her standards."

Snow smiled. Words were all the cowardly little fuck had.

"Dating you?" Snow asked. "I know. But she's trading up."

"My father --"

Snow grabbed his face hard, halting his words. "I don't give a shit who your father is. And if he shows up at Emily's bakery one more goddamn time, he'll be in a world of hurt."

Ian looked a little scared now.

"You are going to go back to wherever the fuck you live now," Snow told him, "and you're going to stay there. Invite your fucking family to visit you next year. I don't care. Just don't fucking come back here. You understand?"

When he released Ian's face, the indignation on it almost had Snow laughing.

"You can't do anything to me!" Ian shouted.

Snow punched him in the nose hard, rocking him in the chair he was taped to. Blood spurted from the man's nose but some of the ire faded from his face.

"There's a lot we can do to you, actually." Snow's tone was menacing. "This is the only warning you're going to get. Leave town. Today. Stay gone. Or you'll be gone."

Ian just stared at him, blood running down his face. The fucker was thinking pretty damn hard. Snow paused, waiting.

"You have something to say?" he asked. "Say it. It's the only shot you're going to get."

"Emily's too good for you," Ian said.

"You're right," Snow replied. "She is. But she's mine. Remember that."

Hero pushed away from the wall. He pulled the man's phone from his jacket. What was left of it, anyway. The boys had smashed it to hell.

"Want us to drop him off?" Hero asked.

Snow nodded. A nice long walk in the cold would do him some good.

"My truck's at the bakery," Ian told them, still bleeding.

"Not anymore," Axel said. "But you shouldn't have too much trouble finding it."

"Thank you, brothers," Snow told them. "I owe you."

Hero shook his head. "Go back to Emily. We've got this."

Snow was just about to turn and do just that. But he wanted one last thing.

Hard as he could, Snow punched Ian in the gut. He wanted to give him something to remember him by.

"Merry Christmas, motherfucker," Snow said.

* * *

Emily

They'd just finished cleaning up when Emily saw Snow's Jeep pull into the parking lot. He was back. It worried her to wonder just what he'd been doing.

She waited inside the back door for him, still wearing the Santa suit. When he spotted her, he pulled her into his arms.

"Want to help an old man get his suit off?" he teased.

Emily smiled, leading him to her office. But once she closed the door, her smile faded. "Ian showed up," she said as he began undoing buttons.

"I know."

"What happened then?" she asked.

"We had a talk," Snow told her, working his way out of the nylon belly that Liza made. Sitting in her office chair, he pulled off the boots. "We came to an understanding."

"An understanding?" Emily wanted to know what he meant by that. And she didn't.

Snow nodded as he took off the red pants, grabbing his jeans and pulling them on.

"He's going to be so mad," she said.

"He was," Snow told her.

"He's going to --"

"He's not going to do *anything*," Snow cut her off. "Promise. It's settled."

Emily wanted to ask what that meant. She really did.

When Snow came around the desk and pulled her into his arms, he pressed a kiss to her forehead. "I know we don't know each other very well. *Yet*. But I need you to trust me where this is concerned. Okay?"

Slowly, she nodded.

"I don't want you to worry about anything except Christmas," Snow told her.

Emily smiled up at him. "I didn't have any plans for Christmas this year."

"Now you do," Snow told her, claiming her mouth in a kiss that had her heart hammering against his. "And if I'm really lucky, you have plans for New Year's, Valentine's Day... All of it."

Jamie Targaet

Jamie Targaet is the author of the Hounds of Hell MC. She's anxious to introduce you to this club of gorgeous, dominant men and the lucky women who surrender to them. The ride is going to get wild at times, not going to lie. But there's thrilling action, scorching hot sex scenes, and all the feels.

Jamie writes erotic romance for Changeling Press, a little fanfiction on the side, and she's an aspiring horror writer in another life. She enjoys time with her family (including the fur babies). She likes good horror movies and shows, emo metal and classic rock, and time spent in other worlds writing and reading. She loves hearing from readers and is looking forward to hearing from you.

Hounds of Hell MC is part of the Hounds of Hell MC Multiverse.

Jamie at Changeling: changelingpress.com/jamie-targaet-a-227

Changeling Press LLC

Contemporary Action Adventure, Sci-Fi, Steampunk, Dark Fantasy, Urban Fantasy, Paranormal, and BDSM Romance available in e-book, audio, and print format at ChangelingPress.com -- MC Romance, Werewolves, Vampires, Dragons, Shapeshifters and Horror -- Tales from the edge of your imagination.

Where can I get Changeling Press Books?

Changeling Press e-books are available at ChangelingPress.com, Amazon, Apple Books, Barnes & Noble, Kobo, Smashwords, and other online retailers, including Everand Subscription and Kobo Subscription Services. Print books are available at Amazon, Barnes and Noble, and by ISBN special order through your local bookstores.

ChangelingPress.com